STITCHES

By

Tom Reimann

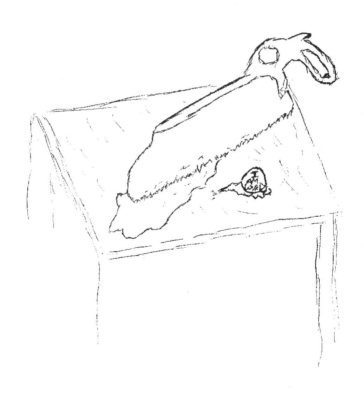

Peter Allan Temple "PETE" b. 14th July, 1985

Date of Recording: 17th October, 2011

Mother's first words: "I love you."

Father's first words: "His head is huge."

Peter's first words: "He-Man."

Takes apart family VCR at age two without damaging a single piece. His father breaks most of the pieces in reassembly.

Enters private school at age 5 after receiving the first ever perfect score on the entrance exam.

Excels in almost every subject, with particular aptitudes in English, Math, and Art. Plays soccer and swims, and is elected class president in both ninth and tenth grade.

Attends Prom for the first time at age 16 after accepting the invitation of an older female classmate who gives him his first drink of alcohol. Disappears from dance after thirty minutes. Is discovered five hours later behind a nearby fast food restaurant, having consumed an entire liter of liquor before engaging in sexual intercourse with one of the restaurant's cashiers. His wallet and one of his shoes are missing, and his tuxedo vest is singed along the bottom edge.

Asked to leave school at age 17 after steady decline in both academic and extra curricular activities, as well as attendance.

Works at a movie theater for three years as a concessions cashier. During this period he keeps a journal of the number of used condoms he finds while cleaning the theaters and frequently inserts his penis into the pre-bagged popcorn.

Earns G.E.D. from community college at age 20. Quits the movie theater and begins working at a sandwich shop.

At age 22, begins to take night classes in creative writing, art, and math at community college. He excels in his studies but seemingly takes courses at random, with no real order towards completion of a degree.

At age 23, moves into an apartment with William August Walker after meeting him in a painting class. Painted mostly abstract landscapes of his own invention, while Walker continually brushed red lines against all-black canvases.

Jillian Archer Edison "JILL" b. 5th August, 1988

Date of Recording: 17th October, 2011

Mother's first words: "Hey there!"

Father's first words: "It's a girl?"

Develops an unnatural fear of *E.T.* at age two after her mother shows it to her on VHS.

Moves away to new state and attends kindergarten, where on her first day a boy spits on her. Learns to read before any of the other children, but keeps this information to herself for fear of being spit on.

At age 5, watches *The Land Before Time* three times a day for an entire year. To date it is her favorite movie.

Moves away to a new state and attends third grade, where on her first day a girl pushes her down for having a "stupid haircut".

Begins writing stories at age 10. Primarily fantasy at first, but quickly graduates into general fiction and horror.

Moves away to new state and attends eighth grade, where on her first day a boy calls her "Wednesday Addams" and draws a picture of her being eaten by a shark.

At age 17, seven of her stories are published in various magazines. Receives a special award from her school, with which her classmates are generally unimpressed.

Attends Junior prom with a disturbingly underweight boy and Senior prom with a disturbingly overweight boy. Both drop her off on a random street corner at the end of the evening after she refuses any sexual advances. Was not able to return either dress.

Graduates in the top tenth percentile of her class and receives several merit awards, which earns scattered applause from her classmates. That evening, attends several parties she is not invited to and, after becoming progressively intoxicated, probably has sex with another girl and two boys in a bathroom. She cannot remember for sure.

Does not attend college and has no future plans to do so. Moves out of state on her own to "figure things out". Shares an apartment with a 29 year old gay waiter she found on Craigslist.

At age 20, consumes a great deal of acid and goes to a public park where she hurls obscenities at a small boy who is taking too long to relinquish his swing. Police intervene and her roommate moves out.

At age 21, moves back into her parents' house. Begins working at a sandwich shop, where she meets Peter Allan Temple. She has not written a story since high school.

William August Walker "AUGER" b. 22nd November, 1984

Date of Recording: 17th October, 2011

Father's first words: "He looks dead."

Mother's first words: "I'm so glad you're here."

Drives car for the first time at age 4, when he steals his mother's keys from her purse while she is in the tub.

Enters preschool at age 5, but is asked to leave four days later after striking another child in the face with his "Scooby-Doo" lunchbox. Subsequently enters and is removed from three more schools, for the reasons given here: "(William's) disturbing, erratic, and often violent behavior makes him incompatible with other children."

Home-schooled until the second grade. During his time at home, he and his parents find ways to distract him and control his behavior. Becomes very skilled at reading, writing, painting, and the dissection of frogs.

Re-enters public school largely without incident at age 7. He and his mother devise a plan to keep him from acting out, which is described here in his own words: "I have a pin I keep in my pocket, and any time I feel angry I'm supposed to grab it and squeeze until I stop being angry." Over subsequent years, demonstrates an incredible aptitude in biological science, which consumes his interest. Graduates from frogs to cats to dogs.

Remains respected member of school community through age 18, though to the best of his mother's knowledge never brought a friend to the house and never went on a date with a girl.

Attends a community college taking pre-med courses with the aspiration of becoming a surgeon. Excels in these courses, but is unable to move onward to medical school for financial reasons. Tires with ultimately fruitless efforts to win any kind of sponsorship or academic scholarship. His life becomes stagnant. He no longer carries a pin.

Pete

One

People don't usually remember their dreams, as is my understanding, but one time when I was about ten or twelve I had a dream about a skeleton bear that I will never forget. There was some kind of dance or ceremony going on with some Indians and a giant bonfire, and this disembodied voice was describing everything I was seeing even though I was seeing it well enough on my own. A dream has its own set of logic ranging anywhere from rational to completely insane, but still you, in the dream, accept every action you witness and every decision you make as perfectly reasonable. Which is why, in the dream, I never bothered to ask myself what I might be doing watching a bunch of Indians and a giant fire.

"*Here,*" the voice booms, "*is where they gathered for the ceremony, celebrating on the graves of their brothers.*" And the Indians do their part, dancing around just like any undereducated white male like me would expect them to. So far, so good.

Then comes the skeleton bear.

"*But there was something else beneath them that day,*" asserts the voice, and just as this sentence is spoken, the aforementioned skeleton bear tears up out of the ground and starts killing him some Indians (I'm being sexist here in selecting a pronoun for the skeleton bear, because nowhere in the dream am I given any clear indication of the skeleton bear's gender).

"*It was,*" the voice continues, "*a bear.*"

I have no idea what this dream means.

Two

I'm not sure why Auger's name is Auger. I doubt his mother named him Auger. In fact, I think his name might be August. Either way, I've never heard of his mother.

I never really see Auger's room. He keeps his door closed when he's home and he keeps it locked when he's not. I try to keep him up to date on things like rent and power, but most times I don't even like to knock on his door. So I leave a note on it instead, which is like knocking only much more passive aggressive. This is not to suggest that Auger is an irritable dickhead; on the contrary, I think we get along pretty well. We hang out and talk and eat dinner together and stuff. I've just always felt this irrepressible urge to respect his privacy.

Auger is at least as old as I am, which is twenty six, but no older than twenty seven, and about as tall as anyone else in that age group. He has straight black hair that spends most of its time hanging in his face, which is clean shaven and pale. I do not know his last name, but I think it's something like Walker or Smith. You wouldn't give it a second glance if you saw it on a mailbox, but that's all I can say for certain. He doesn't talk much, weigh much, or eat any meat. He also doesn't watch television, even though I'm pretty sure the one in our living room is his because it isn't mine. And he does come out and watch movies with me from time to time, so you tell me.

Three

My plan is to get stabbed in the stomach at work so I won't have to go anymore. I'd like for some thief to do it, but most thieves carry guns nowadays, and getting stabbed in the stomach with a bullet typically ends in death. I'm not trying to kill myself. I just want to get a large cash settlement and qualify for disability. I also want people to A) feel sorry for me, and B) think my scar is totally bad ass. If God had wanted us to work, He wouldn't have made all of us hate work so much.

I've thought of paying one of my friends to come in and rob the place, stabbing me in the stomach as they leave with handfuls of cash and salami, but as my friend Nick pointed out, the friend in question would probably get arrested, which makes it difficult for me to convince anyone to go through with it. The only other option is to stab myself when no one is looking. This is not as easy as it sounds.

First of all, I need to find a place at work where I can be alone with a knife. I can't just carry one into the bathroom or something, because our uniforms don't allow for any kind of concealment, unless I want to jam a blade down my pant leg and hope I don't sever an artery. Second, I need a good reason to have a knife sticking out of my belly. Otherwise it would be painfully obvious that I did it myself. Again, this is not as easy as it sounds. Did the knife fall? That's retarded, where the hell would it fall from, *space*? Did someone stab me by accident? Also retarded, when the hell has that ever happened? "Holy shit Pete, didn't see ya there! I was practicing my stabbing and you just jumped outta nowhere!" I suppose I could just hold the tip of the knife at my midsection and run into something, but then how the hell would I explain *that*? Epilepsy? As it stands, I have my goal in mind but no way to achieve it, at least none that I have figured out.

This train of thought brings me to the girl. Every story worth telling has a girl in it. In mine, her name is Jill and she works at The Loaf with me. She's very small and very pretty, and she likes violence and underground radio, which you can tell by looking at her haircut. Her favorite movie is *The Land Before Time*, but I've never seen it so we haven't had a chance to discuss it. Jill and I have a running joke where I tell her to stab me in the stomach so I can punch her in the face and then we can both get sent home. She has no idea I'm serious.

Four

I take sleeping pills, but not to sleep. I set out a bunch on the coffee table in the living room and crush them into powder with a hammer. Auger came out of his room the first time he heard me doing this. He had a little bit of blood on him and a quizzical look on his face, but he didn't say anything. Now he doesn't leave his room when he hears be banging away because he already knows what I'm up to and has no need to come out and confirm it visually. Anyways, I crush up a few pills with the hammer and pour the powder into a glass, which I then fill with Vodka and Mountain Dew. As you may have already guessed, I drink the glass. Then I try to do different things.

I try writing something, or playing video games, or watching a movie. Sometimes I try calling people. I have called Jill on more than one of these occasions, and on more than one of these occasions she has been in the apartment with me drinking the same drink. On more than one of *those* occasions, Auger will come out and talk to us, but he never takes any pills or drinks any drinks that I've seen. He likes violence too. And burritos.

Five

A few months ago, Auger bought a chest freezer to put in the kitchen, which threw me off because how many hot pockets would we realistically ever have to store? I figured the freezer in our fridge was enough for the two of us, it's not like we do a whole lot of sophisticated cooking. We've never even turned our gas on, so the stove in the corner is mostly ornamental. I actually keep books in it.

I asked him why he needed the freezer, but he just kind of gave me that Jared Leto in *Requiem for a Dream* face and said, "Class." I guess he's taking a course in ice cream that I hadn't heard about. At any rate, since then all he's ever put in it is ice. It's full of ice, literally, he can barely close the lid. Strange, yea, but I never bother him about it. I've always felt this irrepressible urge to respect his privacy. I think I mentioned that.

Jill is coming over tonight to bring us dinner she cooked at her house, spaghetti I think. Or she might just steal some food from The Loaf when she gets off, that's what I usually do. We get to work 9 hour days, but we don't get a free meal. Meanwhile, the manager's dumb ass husband comes in all the time and *he* gets to eat for free. Although I guess he deserves it – my manager looks like Candace Bergen if her face got melted off in a chemical fire and she received skin grafts from James Garner's ass. I'd rather stick my dick in a sock full of nails than do anything remotely sexual with that woman, so kudos to husband, I won't begrudge him a free sandwich.

Anyhow, I need to clean this place up a bit, and by "this place" I mean "my face". I feel like I haven't shaved since *Duck Tales* was on television. Jesus, there's that noise again. What the hell is Auger doing in there? I'll just slide a note under his door to remind him about dinner.

Jill

One

The worst dream I ever had was when I was six. I think. Or seven. Either way, it was a long time ago, back when we lived in I guess our second house? Anyway, it was horrible. I dreamt we were getting ready for church, except it was like a movie, you know? Like I wasn't seeing everything as me, I was watching it like it was on television. I hope that makes sense. So we're getting ready for church, and my dad is in one of the guest rooms putting on a sweater, and he reaches his arm up to get it through the sleeve and his hand touches a spider web in the corner.

But the spider web does something to him. Suddenly everything slows down and he sort of reels his hand back down to look at the spider web, and his eyes start glowing. Then I can see out the window behind him, and the sky is red and there's like demons and witches flying by. Not full-on figures, but silhouettes, like shadow puppets you know?

I'm in my room getting dressed, or I'm watching myself getting dressed I mean. Then I hear this noise, and the door explodes open and my dad is standing there. His eyes are red and he's standing incredibly stiff, like a robot. He turns his head very slowly, looking around the room until he sees me. Then Dad stops and points at me and says, "WHY AREN'T YOU READY YET?" But it's not his voice, not really. It's like he's shouting at me from the bottom of a well.

And then I woke up. That was seventeen years ago and I still remember every single detail. I've written it down a bunch before, you know, for myself... god, I sound so crazy. I'm sorry. I'm really sorry.

Two

I'm back living with my parents after three years of being on my own in another state. That says a lot about me, huh? I just got too fucked up on my own and things just sort of got out of control, you know? People keep telling me, "Oh, it just happens sometimes, sweetie, it's nothing to be ashamed of." Right. If it was nothing to be ashamed of, you wouldn't need to say that to me. I'm a waste.

George was nice enough, he got me a job at the same restaurant he worked at, waiting tables just like him. You'd think I would get better tips just because I'm a girl, but *noooo*. People love gay men. He'd have table after table treat him like a novelty, and they'd tip the shit out of him like he was a circus bear or something. Maybe if my boobs were bigger, but oh well. Nothing against him, he was okay. And I still got decent tips, most of the time.

You know the whole fucked up thing about him moving out? *He* was the one that got me doing acid in the first place. I'd never done drugs in my *life* until I moved in with him, but that's like *all he would do*. All the time. Acid, cocaine, whatever. I don't understand how he could afford it, especially since he just gave it to me all the time free of charge. We were definitely the 24 Hour Party People. So one day I go to the playground tripping balls and this little brat kicks sand in my hair and won't get off the swing, so I freak out. Big deal. I said some words he's probably already heard on MTV. I mean he was seriously like ten. It's not like I cussed out a baby in a stroller.

So the cops showed up and took me back to our apartment, and as soon as George sees them he *shits*, probably because he has like nineteen pounds of illegal drugs in the house. But the cops didn't even do anything, they just told me to watch my ass and left me alone. Big deal. But *George* didn't care about all that, just seeing them was enough for him to pack up and leave. He told me, "You're reckless! You're crazy! I can't go to jail! Blah blah blah." What an asshole. So he moves in with his quasi-boyfriend, some guy he screwed in a bathroom at a club like three weeks prior but was "in love" with. Whatever. Anyway, I couldn't keep the place much longer on my own, and I still had to see *George* every day I went to work and he wouldn't even *look* at me. I was barely twenty one and he was like thirty, and he gave me everything I ever took in the first place, so how the hell is it my fault?

So I left. I came back home, I had no money and nowhere else to go. That was two years ago and I'm still here, twenty three and living with my parents. I'm such a waste, I can't stand it.

Three

I'm pretty sure I'm in love with Pete. I met him at The Loaf my first day. It was like two weeks after I'd come back home and I'd applied for the job just because it was close to my house, you know? Anyway, my first day was a closing shift, and he was assigned as my trainer. Even in that first meeting, I could tell I was going to like him a lot. He's really smart and he's funny, and we just had this connection immediately. He told me later that he thought I wasn't in to him at all, because he kept telling these jokes and I wasn't really laughing. The truth was I was so nervous being around him that I just didn't process the jokes right away. Does that make sense? Ugh, I sound like an idiot, I'm sure.

The job itself is kind of lame, but it's not hard and I get paid for it, so I guess that's okay. Better than waiting tables with some backstabbing asshole. Plus I get to hang out with Pete all day, and he's pretty much the only friend I have around here. We just talk about horror movies and music and make fun of the customers. It's actually kind of a blast. I get paid to hang out with my best friend. We have this joke where he says I should stab him so that he can punch me in the face and then we can both go home early. He doesn't know that I would totally stab him and let him punch me in the face if we could go home together. Shit, I think I really do love him. He'd never want me though, not in a million years. I'm so stupid.

Four

I cut myself. Yea, I know, big surprise. The girl with the haircut and all the black and red clothes likes to cut herself. Shocking. It's so pathetically cliché. I don't do it to be dramatic, it's just sometimes I get so mad at myself that… I need to punish myself? God, I sound like a maniac. Forget I said any of that, ok?

I can't write anymore, that's the problem. I've tried, really hard, but I just can't bring myself to actually pound something out. Maybe my ideas aren't any good, maybe I have a motivation problem, I don't know. It's just not happening.

I don't want to kill myself, I hope that's not the impression that I'm giving. It's just sometimes I need to… I don't know. I don't know what I'm saying. I have to admit though, that anytime I feel like I might be getting in too deep into something, like I'm risking a big failure, I comfort myself by thinking, "Hey, if this totally blows up in your face, you can always kill yourself." That's a shitty frame of mind, I know, but sometimes it's the only thing that helps, you know? At least I know I can be in control. Wow, I *am* crazy, aren't I? Pete wouldn't want anything to do with me. I don't know what I was thinking.

Five

It was my choice not to go to college. I just don't see the point, you know? I don't want to wear a suit to work or be a doctor or something. I don't want to be tied down to anything but *me*. If one day I feel the need to just fuck off and leave, I want to be able to do that without having to tender a resignation. I never want to have a job that I can't walk away from at any given moment. That's one of the reasons why I wanted to write for so long, because that's a job you can take with you anywhere you go, screw everything else. Moving away after high school was one of the best things I ever did hands down, even if George did sell me out. And yea, I'll wait tables and live in apartments for the rest of my life if I have to, I don't care. I don't.

Everyone hated me so I left. My parents never cared, no one in my schools ever cared. I tried so hard, too… I really did, I wanted people to like me but they just *didn't* and it's so unfair, you know? What did I ever do to anyone? I'm creative! I'm… I'm a little pretty, I think… I wrote all these stories and a bunch of them got published, but no one I know ever read them. No one ever came up to me with "Hey, good work!" or "I saw your story" or even "That shit fucking sucked". Nobody cared about anything I did.

Six

So my dad bought this new TV a few days ago. It's a big flatscreen, like 52 inches, and it hangs on the wall. It's actually kind of cool, you know? For movies and stuff. I want to invite Pete and Auger over to watch *The Land Before Time* on it, because I know Pete hasn't seen it even though he sort of pretends like he saw it once a long time ago. And Auger… I feel like he needs to get out, you know? I don't think he has any friends besides Pete. I mean, neither do I, not really, but Auger doesn't even have a *phone*. It's like he doesn't *want* to have any friends. But I think he'd like the movie, you know? Who doesn't like dinosaurs?

I'm actually going over there tonight and bringing them dinner, because those two never cook anything for themselves that they can't microwave. They never even turned on their *gas*, so it's like an impossibility for them to, you know, roast a chicken or something. Anyway, I'm bringing spaghetti with tomato sauce and red peppers and carrots, and some burritos for Auger. I know he'll eat the spaghetti, there's no meat in it, but I think he'll like the extra gesture. I want him to feel like people want to be his friend, because I know what it's like to not have any. I hope that makes sense. Anyway, he doesn't have to eat them tonight, he can save them for lunch or something, they'll be fine in the fridge for a few days I think.

I cut myself a little deep today, I didn't mean to, it just happened. I was thinking about George and high school and, like, just all these things that I want to do but I just *haven't*, you know? I tried to move away but I fucked that all up and crashed right back home, right where everyone thought I was going to end up, and I can't write anything anymore and I don't have any *friends* and... I just want... I just want to go. I want somebody to go with, though, somebody that won't leave me? Or freak out, I guess? I just want someone to *care*... oh, whatever. Nobody gives a shit about me anyway.

Dinner

Pete shaves in time for dinner, but tries to move too fast and suffers a few cuts which he blots up with tissues. As he is walking past Auger's door to the common room, the door opens, which startles him. Auger stares at him expressionlessly for a moment, then moves out of the doorway and closes the door behind him.

"Are we still having dinner?" Auger asks.

"Yea," Pete says. "Jill is bringing it over in a few. Spaghetti I think. Or she might just steal some stuff from work, I dunno."

Auger says nothing.

"Is that... is that cool?" Pete asks.

"Yes that's cool," Auger says. He walks past Pete into the common room and sits down on the couch.

"Are you okay?" Pete asks him.

Auger doesn't seem to hear for a moment, then turns his head slowly to look at Pete and respond. "Yes I'm fine. Should we watch a movie?"

Pete shrugs. "Sure, if you want. It's not like we have a table, we're going to be eating out here anyway. What do you feel like watching?"

Auger looks at Pete for a long time without blinking. "Something you and Jill will enjoy," he says finally.

"Ah, ok, well Jill and I are going to enjoy anything from *Cool Runnings* to Dario Argento, so speak now or forever hold your peace," Pete says with a smile.

"*Suspiria*," Auger says immediately. "That should go well with spaghetti, I think."

Pete blinks. "Okay. Awesome choice. I'll go get it."

Pete goes into his bedroom to retrieve the *Suspiria* DVD right as Jill knocks on the door. Auger rises from the couch and crosses the common room to answer.

"Hey Auger!" Jill says as the door is opened. She is holding two porcelain containers covered with aluminum foil, but still manages to lean up and kiss Auger on the cheek. "Hope you're hungry, because I brought enough food to choke a *whale*."

Auger nods. "I'm hungry," he says, and takes one of the containers from Jill and lets her inside.

Pete comes out from his bedroom with the DVD in hand. "Hey Jillybean!" he says, and he walks over to hug her.

"Hey buddy," Jill says mid-hug. They break the embrace and look at each other for a moment. Auger watches, shifting the container from one hand to the other.

"Well!" Jill says finally. "Let's eat this shit!"

Pete laughs. "Okay. Let's put this shit in the microwave first, I like my shit hot."

Thirty minutes later they are sitting on the couch, Auger next to Pete next to Jill, watching *Suspiria* with plates in their laps.

"Hey, are the burritos okay? I thought maybe you could save them and eat them for lunch tomorrow or something?" Jill asks Auger.

Auger looks at her, then looks back at the t.v. "Yes, I'll probably eat them later tonight or tomorrow for breakfast or lunch," he says. "Thank you."

"Well that's what friends are for, right?" Jill says.

Auger does not respond. "Your wrist is bleeding," he says finally.

Jill draws her arm into herself and looks panicky first at Auger and then at Pete. "I... I caught myself when I was cutting up the vegetables," she says. "Stupid. But I'm fine, really."

Pete asks, "Are you okay? Can I see?"

"No!" Jill says, shrinking back a little. "No. It's... nothing, I'm fine, really I promise. I just snagged myself, that's all, no big deal right?"

Silence. Auger says, "I can sew you up. I can fix it."

Jill trembles, "Auger please, it's not a big deal, I'm fine."

"But you're bleeding," Auger says.

Pete says, "Auger, leave it alone. She's fine, it's just a cut, right?"

Jill nods. "Yea," she says. "It's just... just a cut."

"It hasn't stopped bleeding the entire night," Auger says. "I can give you some gauze and tape if you prefer, but I want you to stop bleeding."

Pete says, "Auger..."

Jill interrupts, "Okay."

Silence. Pete looks at Jill, who looks right back at him. Then Pete looks at Auger, who is looking only at Jill. Auger says, "Hold on" and he stands up and goes into his bedroom.

Pete says to Jill, "Are you okay with this? He can be a little weird, you don't have to let him give you a bandage."

Jill says, "I know, but I think I need it actually. There's no reason not to put a bandage on a cut, you know? I was just being stupid."

Auger walks back into the common room with some gauze and medical tape, and a bottle of alcohol and cotton swabs. He sits down on the couch next to Jill. "Give me your wrist," he says.

Jill hesitates.

"Jill," Auger says. "Please give me your wrist."

Jill stretches her hand out to Auger, who takes it and rolls her sleeve up. There is a deep gash across her wrist, pushing blood out over countless other scars on her arm. Pete inhales audibly. Jill starts to cry a little.

"You cut a lot of vegetables," Auger says. He cleans the cut with alcohol and wraps a strip of gauze around Jill's wrist.

Jill hangs her head very low and begins to cry harder. "I'm sorry," she sobs. Pete wraps his arms around her and holds her tightly, repeating, "It's okay, don't worry, everything's fine…"

Auger does not respond.

An hour and a half later, Jill is leaving the apartment. Pete is making sure she takes the empty container that held the spaghetti home with her.

"Would you walk me out?" Jill asks Pete as she stands in the open doorway. "It's kind of late, you know?"

Pete smiles and says, "Yea of course, I can do that."

Pete walks to his room to get a coat and then comes back out to the entryway. "Be back in two seconds," he says to Auger, who stands in the common room watching them leave.

"G'nite Auger," Jill says as she walks over to hug Auger and kiss him on the cheek. "Thanks," she says.

Auger nods. Jill and Pete walk outside and close the door.

Auger waits ten seconds, then enters the kitchen. He opens the chest freezer and digs through the ice for a moment before pulling out a human hand, severed at the wrist. He closes the chest freezer and crosses the apartment to his bedroom, locking the door behind him.

Jill

One

I really made an idiot of myself at Pete and Auger's the other night. I knew I should've wrapped my wrist up before I left, it was bleeding so much, but I guess part of me wanted them to see. Does that make sense? Ugh, I'm such a mess. They probably both think I'm crazy and they'll stay my friends for a little bit longer just because they feel *sorry* for me and then I'll never see them again, because that's what people do when they find out you've got *problems*. I'll never forget this one time with George, it was like three in the morning and we'd been up all night doing massive amounts of coke and drinking wine coolers. I thought my heart was going to explode. Anyways, we're alternating between watching episodes of *Family Guy* and comparing our body parts, and we're pretty much both naked but in a completely non sexual way. We're like comparing *elbows* and weird things like that, and plus George is so totally gay I think he would rather *die* than touch a vagina. So we're comparing our thighs and he notices that I've got some pretty deep scars on them, and then he looks at my wrists and sees *those* scars, and I've also got a few on my stomach… anyway, he sees them and he flips out. He's all like, "Oh no, you're one of those *emo* girls that cuts on herself! Jesus, why don't you go back to LiveJournal with that shit!" Which is total crap because gay men loved LiveJournal and George totally had one, so I don't know what choir he thought he was preaching to. So he gets like *mad* at me, like really pissed off, and I start crying so he calms down a bit and tells me to do more cocaine to "cheer me up", and then goes in the back to the bathroom, and at this point I just feel like absolute utter *shit*, like toxic waste, and the drugs *aren't* cheering me up so I grab a razor blade off the coffee table and *stab* it into my skin and drag it along my wrist and just sit there and bleed and cry, sitting in my panties and socks on the floor just *leaking*. It must've been like fifteen minutes before George came back and I don't know what he took while he was in the bathroom but he didn't notice the blood at all, or if he did he was too jacked up to have any meaningful reaction. So we sit out there for the rest of the night, I think. I don't really remember much after that.

Two

So today at work we had a meeting where we all had to sit out in the dining room and watch some video about teamwork and workplace hospitality and stuff. I actually kind of like when we have meetings because Pete always finds a way to sit next to me but make it awkward at the same time, like he'll wait until the last minute to come find a seat and he *knows* its going to be the seat next to me because *everyone* knows that's where Pete wants to sit so nobody ever takes it. It's adorable. I mean, we spend all day practically attached at the hip, but suddenly at movie time he needs to find an *excuse* to sit next to me? *Other* than the fact that we're friends and we talk all day *anyway*? It'd be frustrating if it wasn't so endearing, I think. So we watched the movie and it was retarded and Pete and I made jokes the entire time, and I started to feel better about the other night, you know? It doesn't seem like he feels any differently about me, he's not asking me if I'm okay every fifteen seconds and he's not being weird or distant or anything. He's just being Pete, and that's awesome. That really makes me happy. I hope Auger isn't mad at me about it. It was really kind of sweet, honestly, when he insisted on giving me a bandage. I should've *known* he would notice the blood, he's a *doctor*, basically. Anyway, I hope he's not mad, especially not after I went through all that trouble bringing him burritos so he'd want to be my friend. I think I'm going to have to make a burrito *cake* to make up for it.

Three

My mom and dad don't really bother me, now that I'm back at home. They ask me the standard parent questions, like "How are you doing?" and

"How's the job coming?" and things like that, but really we don't see each other, like, ever. When I'm home I pretty much just stay in my room and they don't come knocking, you know? Which is cool I guess, I'm not a teenager anymore and it's not like I act out or anything, so they really don't have any reason to wonder what I'm up to these days. I'm pretty much a homebody lately anyhow, so they don't even need to worry about me waking them up when I come home at all hours of the night because I'm usually home before they go to bed.

Pete's spent the night a couple of times before, but totally not in a sexual way, just like two friends sleeping over, you know? I mean, he sleeps in the bed with me, but like I'm in my pajamas and he sleeps above the sheets, so it's totally fine. One time he sat on my floor and read me some old book, I think it was *The Screwtape Letters*, but he was doing this *goofy* voice like a spastic Jimmy Stewart and it was *hilarious*, and he sat there and read that book for like an *hour* because I was laughing so hard. He's pretty great. I hope he's not mad at me. He's suggested before that we should try writing something together, since we both like to write and I've actually had some things published, but I don't know what we would write. His stuff, what I've read of it anyway, is mostly like humor pieces, and I don't really write funny. Still, it might be fun to try… god, I hope I didn't screw everything up the other night. I really do, because Pete… I want him to be the one that I can leave with, you know? I really want it to be him. When he sleeps over we always wind up like cuddled together the next morning, but I don't think he realizes that I wake up in the middle of the night and just… wrap myself around him, sort of. I'm so stupid, he'd never move away with me, I'm just a dumb *"tragic"* girl that cuts herself when she's sad. Wow, it really sounds melodramatic when you say it like that.

Four

Ok, so there's this guy that comes into The Loaf like twice a week and orders a quart of chicken noodle soup, but he wants it *broth only*, none of the titular chicken or noodles. The soup is pre-made though, we have bags of it in the freezer that we just thaw as needed, so when this ass-hat comes in we have to sit there and ladle all of the non-liquid ingredients out of a quart of soup. It doesn't bother me too much, but it's *amazing* to see how pissed Pete gets at this guy. I'll agree it's asinine and tedious, but Pete is ready to knock this dude's *teeth* out over some chicken broth. It makes me laugh.

There's also this guy that comes in every day and just loads up a bag full of our free samples. Pete calls him Foggle. We cut up bread or pastries or something every morning and set them out on a tray in the lobby for people to try, and then Foggle comes in and dumps a whole bunch of them into a canvas bag and then leaves. We know he's not homeless because we've seen him driving a car and he has nice clothes and stuff. So today, Pete decides he's going to steal Foggle's bag, which should be easy because the one other thing this guy takes advantage of is our bathroom. Three days out of the week when he comes in to collect our free samples, he'll make a fifteen minute detour in the bathroom. *And he never flushes.* Then he'll come out and tell us that the toilet's stopped up. So anyways, today he goes into the bathroom and leaves his bag at one of the tables, and as soon as the bathroom door closes Pete like *sprints* around the counter and grabs the bag and runs into the back with it and we start going through it, giggling like idiots. And this guy has *everything*, like bagels and old pretzels and hot dogs and just *anything* that any of the restaurants in the neighborhood hand out or throw away in the morning, plus a bunch of yesterday's newspapers and like a full stack of unused coffee cups from 7-11 which really confuses me. Maybe he broke all his coffee mugs or something.

Anyway, Pete wants to just throw the bag away now that we've seen it, but I felt a little bad about it so we decide to put it back, but before we put it back we each take a pen and draw little pictures on the side of every single coffee cup. Pete's a pretty good artist, he was drawing all these ridiculous things like a toaster with a broadsword and a bowl of macaroni and cheese jumping rope. It was *amazing*. The best part is, we take all this time drawing pictures and when we finally put the bag back on the table we think it's like a *photo finish*, but Foggle is in the damn bathroom for like ten more minutes after that. I almost made Pete go see if he'd *died* in there. I bet he never even notices the pictures.

Five

Pete missed work today, so it was totally lame. I was stuck on soups with this asshole named Jake who's like 18 and tries way too hard to try to hit on me all the time. All he talks about is smoking weed and his clothes *reek* of it, and he's *dumb* as a rock and tells these stupid ass jokes that *nobody* ever laughs at. Ugh. And he's always trying to talk to me and we have absolutely *nothing* in common. I told him that I've written stories for magazines one time and it almost fucked his tiny brain to death, like he couldn't imagine girls doing anything but drinking and going to clubs with him and his dumb ass friends. I *vote* too, asshole. How about *them* apples?

Anyways, so we run out of like French onion right in the middle of lunch because Jake forgot to put any out to thaw, and then everyone starts yelling at *me* because I'm the more experienced one and should've been paying more attention and all this other garbage. It's like, he had *one job* and that was to thaw the soups, and suddenly it's *my* fault because he can't even figure that out? Ugh, I'm so over today. I think I'm going to go home and punch my goddamn wall or something.

Six

I really wish I could start writing again. Like, it never really *relaxed* me or anything, but it gave me something to fill up the days, you know? After school and everything. Like, I mean, I'd hang out sometimes too, I had *some* friends… but no one I've really kept in touch with. I don't have any idea where anyone from high school is right now. I just spent most of my time by myself, and it maybe wasn't the most "well-adjusted" thing I could've done but I felt like I was doing something that kind of mattered a little, like in the cosmic sense. I always get this feeling when I read stuff that's been written by people that died like a hundred years ago, that they've been able to graduate from just *people* into something more. Does that make sense? I don't think I'm explaining it very well. What I mean is, if you read something by Stephen King you can go online and send him an email about it, but with someone like Christopher Marlowe, you can't. He made his mark and now he belongs to eternity. He exists in your head because of some ideas he decided to write down on paper like four hundred years ago, so now you read it and it's like he's talking to you even though he's *dust*. I want to be able to do that. I want to be able to reach out to people that haven't even been *born* yet, you know? It's... it means a lot to me, I hope it makes sense. I want to be more than "the girl at The Loaf". I want my contribution to the human experience to be more than Jake sitting at home jacking off because he managed to see the top of my underwear at work today. I want people to remember me after I die because it's not like anyone remembers me *now*... but I don't even have any good ideas to write about.

I feel like I'm running out of time, you know? I know it sounds kind of crazy, I mean I'm barely 23, but I'm still so scared of never doing anything with my life that means something. Like, I'm literally *scared*. I'm back in my parents' house, my life is blowing up in my face... what the hell am I doing? And people don't like me, Pete and Auger are probably freaked out because of my *wrist*, I can't be creative anymore but it's not like anyone ever cared when I *was*... I really tried to be great, I did. I want to be so good, you know? Just so good for everything, and go to amazing places and meet people and have *conversations* and just be happy. I feel like I'm missing my only chance, you know? I'm only 23 but pretty soon I'll be 30 and I want to have an answer for that. I want to be able to say, "Kiss my ass, I'm so fucking awesome your head will explode!" to everyone I meet... well, maybe not the "kiss my ass" part if I'm trying to make friends, but you get it, I think. Except I'm not that person, and I don't know how to be. Ugh. Maybe Jake will show up and masturbate at my funeral for the eulogy.

Shit. I just hit myself pretty hard, my nose is bleeding. I wish I could call Pete right now but I don't know what to say to him, you know? I can't just be like, "Pete help me, I'm hurting myself and I can't stop"... how would he even *respond* to that? God, I'm so crazy. I hate you Jill, I hate you so much… oh… oh, no… that, that was a little silly Jill why would you do that? God, I'm really bleeding, oh no, oh no, oh no…

Pete

One

I have this idea for a book where I'd just write it as an action movie, complete with inexplicable explosions and witty banter, and probably one or two lasers on the moon and maybe a dinosaur. And I'd deliberately make the plot the most nonsensical thing in the history of the world, something to the effect of "Terrorists hijack a milk truck and only Jean Claude van Damme's stepbrother's friend Mitch can stop them!" I think there's a huge market for this just waiting to *explode*. Get it? Explode? See, this is a gold mine.

So, the thing with Jill… it doesn't bother me, at least not in the sense that it makes me want to spend less time around her. I don't think she's a psycho or anything like that. Far be it from me to pass judgment on other people, especially not someone who's essentially my best friend. I don't think she's crazy at all, she's smart and funny and creative. But I have to admit, the other night really messed me up. It made me very sad, because I like Jill a lot. Pretty things shouldn't have to bleed like that. I actually cried, if you can believe it. After I walked her out and we said our goodbyes and carefully tap danced around actually discussing the issue of her having obviously mutilated herself, I came back in and sat on the couch and started bawling. Really sobbing, just crying like a baby. Surprisingly, Auger didn't come out of his room, though I think he must have heard me. I know I paint sort of a weird picture of him, but that's just *Auger*. He's… well, he's weird. But he's my roommate and he's my friend, and he normally comes out if he hears me up and about. Unless he's working on something, which I assume he must have been.

At any rate, with no one to talk to and nothing to get the image of Jill's bloody scars out of my mind, I did what any intellectual would do – I got *stupid drunk*. Horribly, horribly drunk was I. I think I might have even tried to call Jill, but I can't remember. And, as per my normal ritual, I took quite a few crushed up sleeping pills, which does fantastic things for your liver, I'm sure. I woke up the next morning in my bed with my right hand bandaged up in gauze. This is the first time something like this has ever happened to me. When I took the bandage off, I saw a row of four stitches across my palm holding together what looked like a considerably awful wound.

Of course it was Auger, who else could it have been? Still, even given the mystery wound on my hand that he had obviously sewn up for me, I couldn't bring myself to actually *knock on his door*. So I wrote him a note and slipped it underneath.

Two

So today was meeting day at work, where we all get corralled into the dining room after hours and watch a video that typically informs us how we're underperforming in one way or another. It's really terrific, it truly puts the staff at ease. I took my usual seat next to Jill, but I always do this thing where I try not to make it obvious that I want to sit next to her. I have no idea why I do this, everyone at The Loaf knows we're retarded for each other, so there's no reason for me to pretend otherwise except to satisfy some ridiculous notion of my own invention. So I sat next to her like I always do and we had fun, we made dumb jokes to keep each other laughing, but it was killing me to be sitting there and not be talking to her about how she hurts herself. I just wanted to grab her by the shoulders like Clark Gable and tell her that she should call me anytime that happens, anytime she starts getting the feeling like she's going to cut into her skin with a razor blade she should just *call me* and I'll help her. I'll drop whatever I'm doing and I'll go to her and I'll *help*, I don't know how but I'll do it. Maybe with ice cream.

Three

I haven't seen Auger in a few days, actually not since the three of us had dinner. So consequently, the mystery of my stitched-up hand remains just that, which is a shame because I'd really like to know what the hell happened to it. Not enough to knock on Auger's door, but still, it's been nagging me.

Classes are starting to get boring, unfortunately. This is astounding to me, because even after taking almost four years off from school I still have no idea what direction I want my life to go in. Maybe I should take more time off, I don't know. My friend Nick thinks I need to just pack up and leave, that a dramatic change of scenery would be the best thing for me. I think he might be right. The only problem is I have no idea where I would go. Also, I'd hate to leave Jill, and not just because of what happened at dinner. At any rate, I'm losing interest in college, which is very disheartening. Especially since it's costing me money. My "getting stabbed at work" plan really needs to come to fruition sooner rather than later. Maybe I can just deliberately shortchange a drug dealer and leave him a note with my Loaf schedule.

Four

Today at work Jill and I played a prank on this guy that comes in all the time and takes our free samples. He never buys anything, but he *does* make a thrice-weekly donation in our bathroom, so at least he gives a little back. He carries a big sack around with him everywhere he goes and he has the same expression fixed on his face at all times, like someone farted in his mouth but he doesn't know who. Picture Foggle from *Labyrinth* and you've got him.

So Foggle shuffles in this morning after we've been open for maybe thirty minutes and sweeps half the tray of samples (which today are apple pastries) into his bag. Then he scuttles off to a table and sits, making sure to take a newspaper from our rack without paying for it. I can't be too hard on Foggle for that though - most of our customers think that if they just take a paper to read while they're here and leave it at the table when they're done, no money needs to change hands. This frustrates me to no end. I know the papers only cost 50 cents but it's the principle of the thing, and most of the people that come to The Loaf can spare two extra quarters to go with their nine dollar lattes. I mean, I wouldn't come to someone's birthday and assume that it's okay to open one of their presents as long as I don't take it with me.

The contents of Foggle's bag have weighed heavily on me ever since I first saw him come in and loot our pastry tray. After all, his resemblance to a goblin from a fantasy movie urgently suggests that there might be treasure of some kind inside, maybe some magical items like an ice scepter or a gilded dagger. Or maybe Amelia Earhart. There was no way to be certain. Naturally, I decided to steal it, and this morning I finally got my opportunity.

After nestling himself into a table with a bunch of unpaid merchandise, he gets up to shamble off to the bathroom for one of his porcelain-splitting thunderdumps that I somehow always manage to have to mop up. With Jill as my lookout, I sprint over, snatch the bag, and carry it to the back undetected. Sadly, as it turns out all that's in the bag is a bunch of crap Foggle took from all the *other* restaurants on our block, no treasure, magic or missing aviators. I'm about to throw the whole thing away in my disappointment, but Jill wisely stops me and we come up with a better idea – there's inexplicably a stack of unused coffee cups from 7-11 in the bag, so we draw pictures on every single one. My only regret is that I don't get to experience Foggle's confusion upon seeing a shark with a jetpack when he pours his morning coffee.

Five

Auger finally shows up today while I'm sitting in the common room eating breakfast before work. He comes in with a plastic garbage bag in his hand and walks straight into his room and closes the door without saying a word to me. I assume he must be working on something since I haven't seen him in three days and he doesn't seem to be interested in making conversation. So I turn my attention back to my Cinnamon Toast Crunch. Surprisingly, I hear Auger's door open again after only a few minutes, and he walks out into the common room and sits on the couch with me.

"Hey Auger," I say. "What's up?" Auger doesn't respond immediately, he seems to be considering something. This isn't unusual for Auger so I don't think anything of it. Finally he says, "You cut your hand."

I stare at him for a moment. "Yea," I say. "Yea I did. I don't remember how, though. Do you know, did you see me do it? I'm assuming you stitched it up for me."

Auger nods. "You grabbed a kitchen knife out of the drawer by the blade," he says. "It cut half a centimeter deep into your palm."

So that's what happened. "Ah," I say to Auger. "Well thanks for cleaning it up for me, man." Auger doesn't respond. He still seems to be considering something. I never ask him about it when he gets like this, because as I've said I feel an irrepressible urge to respect his privacy. So I get up to take my bowl into the kitchen and leave for work. In the kitchen, I put the bowl in the sink and run some water into it to wash the milk down the drain. When I turn around, Auger is standing in the doorway.

"Uh, what's... what's up, Auger?" I say. I can't get the words out right away because he has startled me a little.

Auger says, "Stand still."

Before I can ask why, Auger's arms lash out at me so fast I can barely discern anything but two slender blurs. I feel his hand on my shoulder pushing me forward a bit and then he punches me in the stomach, forcing the air out of my lungs. I try to move away from him, but instead I feel myself falling against him. There is a horrible pain in my stomach now, an invasive feeling, and I still can't move as Auger lowers me down to the kitchen floor. My shirt is soaking wet and I don't understand at first until I finally manage to bend my neck very slightly to look and realize that Auger hasn't punched me at all. He squats down next to me and the floor around his shoes is turning red and I can't see very well right now, sort of like when you stand up too fast and everything gets dark, and I say, "Auger... why... why did..." and the last thing I see is Auger's genuine confusion at this question.

Auger

One

My room smells like old blood, that copper scent which only certain people recognize, be it from their line of work or choice of leisure. The walls and carpet are covered with plastic sheeting for the sake of both efficiency and our security deposit. In the center of the room is an operating table that I bought at an auction for 300 dollars. It is only a few years old, and I've maintained it well, so it still shines with the same luster that I imagine it ever had. I never use the overhead light – instead, I have several standing lamps with soft glowing bulbs that illuminate blue-white in whatever direction I position them. There is a tray for my tools and a cot in the far corner for me to sleep on. I have no other furniture. I keep my clothes in a box in the closet.

I had a dream when I was five that I was laying facedown in my bed and a ghost with no face was relentlessly slashing at my back, tearing into my shoulders and my legs, flying horribly above me like a shredded bedsheet blowing crazily in the wind. I never sleep on my stomach now. I want to see him coming.

Two

Pete never knocks on my door. He always writes me notes and slides them inside my room. It seems like he is constantly afraid of me. I've done everything I know how to keep him comfortable – I sit with him, I eat with him, I bought a television for the apartment and I come out and watch movies with him. He still never seems completely at ease around me, which is troubling. I've never had a friend before, and I believe Pete is my friend, so I don't want him to be afraid of me. After all, he has no reason to be. There is nothing about me that is the least bit frightening. I believe Jill is my friend as well, and she doesn't seem to be uneasy around me at all, which is encouraging. She and Pete get along so well that I'd hoped her opinion of me might help assuage whatever worry Pete is feeling, but so far that hasn't happened. He drinks with sleeping pills for fun, which is horrible for his liver and could possibly cause him to drown in his own vomit, but I don't want to increase his unease with me by trying to lecture him. He seems very intelligent so I assume he knows the risks associated, although recently I began replacing his pills with placebos and he has yet to notice.

Three

    This subject was interesting, something I had read about in a detective novel. Blunt force trauma to the head, which I dealt with a hammer, and the right hand severed at the wrist, which I accommodated with my bone saw. Middle aged white male, easy to find, I waited behind a dumpster in the parking lot of a bar and discovered one soon enough, alone, unlikely to struggle and further injure himself. Both wounds were delivered on the operating table to ensure precise control and positioning. In the novel the victim was not found until three hours after the attack, so I put the subject's hand on ice and restrained him.

    Jill's dinner was very good. She brought me burritos as well, I suspect as a gesture to solidify our relationship. It's puzzling, I have never been fond of anyone, yet I find myself enjoying the time I spend with Jill and Pete. My mind relaxes. I'm able to pull myself away from work, if even just for a while. She was bleeding tonight. I could smell it as soon as she walked inside and I noticed her sleeve was damp around the wrist when I took one of her dishes. I didn't want to say anything at first, but she made a remark about friendship, and I assumed that a friend of Jill's would tell her that she was bleeding so I did, because I believe we are friends. She recoiled, which told me immediately that she had injured herself deliberately and I normally have no interest in those types of subjects. But still I asked if she would let me help her, and she eventually agreed to some gauze in lieu of actual stitches, which when I finally saw the wound I decided she would most certainly need. There were seventeen scars scattered around her wrist and I imagine her other arm looks much the same way, a pale desert with old canyons carved across the landscape by the hand of God Herself. She started to cry, perhaps from the alcohol swab I applied to the cut but more likely out of shame. I normally have no interest in this either, tears of self pity disgust me to the point of nausea, but tonight I felt something different. It reminded me of a time I met a young lady beneath an overpass that had slipped and fallen onto rebar. She was on the ground, one leg straight out in front of her and the other tucked beneath, with one metal rod through her stomach an inch to the left of her belly button and another through her chest just above her heart. I knelt beside her and introduced myself, to which she did not respond but her eyes were already glassy so I wasn't offended. I explained the extent of her injuries and offered my assistance, though at this point I was certain she would die within the next ten minutes with or without my help. Then she started to cry. No words, just gasping sobs and an endless stream running down her face. As I said, I typically loathe self pity, but this was different. Every thought was wiped from my mind and all I could do was sit down next to her and watch. She cried for a long time, blood was starting to come out of her mouth and her nose, and she reached a hand towards me, barely able to lift it more than a few inches off the ground. I didn't know what she wanted so I just stared at her hand until it fell down into the dirt and when I looked back at her face she had died. This is the same way I felt when Jill began to cry tonight. It's very troubling for me.

After Jill and Pete left, I retrieved the subject's hand and went about reattaching it to his body. I had just started preparing for the procedure when the subject began vomiting on himself. Fearing he would asphyxiate, I removed his restraints and turned his head, scooping the vomit out of his mouth with my fingers. As I did so, he tried to speak to me but it was nonsense. His eyes were flicking about rapidly and seeing nothing, which heightened his panic. I tried to restrain him again but he was struggling forcefully, bleeding from his nose and from the wound on his head, and I finally noticed a mass of what looked like oatmeal sliding through his hair and onto the table and I knew he was going to die. I released him and he tumbled onto the floor, grey matter splattering across the plastic like spilled gruel. Retrieving the bone saw from my tray of tools, I severed his spine at the base of his neck and he stopped moving. I intend to compose a strongly worded letter to the author of that detective novel. He obviously did no research whatsoever.

Four

Collecting my fees can be difficult at times, depending on the subject. The easiest way is to purchase a money order from a convenience store using the subject's credit card. The clerks never ask for identification and the money order can only be traced to the point where it's collected, which I do immediately. I never visit the same locations more than once every eight months and I frequently travel several hours outside of the city to cast a wider operating radius for myself. Other times I am able to accept cash directly from the subject, should they be carrying an adequate amount. Due to certain constraints my fees must always be paid up front, before I do any work on the subject. I have received the odd complaint, but usually there are no objections.

I mentioned I had replaced Pete's pills with placebos, but the night of Jill's dinner I switched them again for something much more potent that what he normally takes. I did this as an anticipatory measure because the procedure I was attempting was going to be a challenge, and in the event of failure I didn't want Pete to be alarmed by what he might hear or see. As it turns out this was a wise decision. While I was cleaning up the subject's corpse I heard Pete come back into the apartment and start crying loudly in the common room. Something must have upset him, which worked to my advantage because he wouldn't be able to hear anything above his own sobs and therefore would be unlikely to detect anything coming from my room that might cause further worry. As I said, he seems to be constantly afraid of me, so I do my best not to agitate him. Eventually the crying stopped, and after a moment I heard the telltale banging of a hammer signaling the beginning of a night of intoxication. By the time I had replaced the plastic in my room, Pete had crushed up two more pills to put in his drink. He was rapidly approaching a very dangerous level, but I couldn't hold Pete entirely responsible because he didn't realize the potency of what he was taking. Content that my table and all my instruments were clean and the subject was properly secured for removal, I went into the common room to keep an eye on him in case he overdosed, except he wasn't in the common room. I found him in the kitchen holding one of the ten inch carving knives by the blade, blood seeping through his clenched fingers and running down the handle onto the tiled floor. I asked him what he was doing and he could offer no coherent response at first aside from a single word I was able to pick out of his gibberish: "Practice." I asked him what he was practicing for, and gradually he became more lucid and was able to tell me that he wanted to get stabbed in the stomach at work so he could collect a large settlement and never have to go back, and he asked me where in his stomach would cause the least amount of serious or permanent injury. This is not as easy as it sounds. I convinced him to let me stitch up his hand and walked him to his bed, where he promptly passed out. I turned his head to one side in case he should vomit and left him alone.

Back in my room I had the subject to deal with. I'd separated him into seven carefully wrapped bundles, so I carried each bundle down one at a time and loaded them into Pete's car. I then disposed of them in seven separate cities adjacent to our own, all the while thinking about Pete's question. I should have an answer for him fairly soon.

Jill

One

I wake up in the bathtub and I'm naked but there's no water, my arms are wet but there's nothing in the tub? Oh... oh, I'm bleeding... my wrist, I've cut it too deep this time, I must've passed out. I try to sit up but I'm so lightheaded I can't focus on anything. I can't remember how I even got in the tub, I was standing in front of the mirror, I punched myself in the face a few times I think, then I cut... I don't think I was naked, how did that happen? And I definitely wasn't in the bathtub. God, the whole tub is red I think, I need to wrap something around my wrist. Oh no Jill what did you do? Mom and Dad aren't home, what are you going to do? I can't call 9-1-1, I don't want them to find out.

I finally manage to pull myself half out of the tub, I'm sort of laying with my stomach on the rim and my face and arms touching the bathroom floor, blood is running into my face now and I can feel it in my hair. I'm so weak I can hardly move, I'm pushing with my legs now, slowly coming out of the tub but my shoulder is against the toilet and it's getting harder to force my way out, oh Jill sweetie this isn't good, not at all, I'm seeing spots now and my head is feeling heavy and I'm gone again.

Two

Light? What is that... it's the overhead light in the bathroom. I'm on my back with my legs propped up against the side of the tub. I feel like I'm under water, like I'm floating, rocking back and forth in the ocean or something. I throw up suddenly, violently, and for a moment I can't turn my head and I start to panic, then finally I roll my head to the side and spit everything out, gasping, ugh it's in my nose and the floor has red smeared all over it. Oh. Now I remember. I look down to the cut on my wrist and I'm ghost white, like a bedsheet, and I start to cry but feebly because I feel so weak, like when you wake up from a hard nap in the middle of the day if that makes sense. Oh no I don't want to die, I really don't, not yet... Jill I'm so sorry. If I can get a towel and tie it around my arm maybe I'll be okay, there's one by the sink.

I push with my elbows until I'm on my stomach and I start trying to crawl across the room, I'm moving very slow and I have to slide through my puke, I don't even think I can smell it right now but my face is in it and I throw up again. I lay still for a minute or maybe ten minutes, I can't tell, just sort of breathing in a puddle of my own vomit. Pete would never talk to me again if he could see me now, I look like Nancy Spungen. Finally I'm moving again, I'm literally pulling myself along with my fingertips and I'm so white I look like a freaking *snowman*, I've made it to the sink and now I'm holding onto the pedestal stem at the bottom like it's my mother and I'm just breathing for now and even that's getting harder.

I tilt my head a little and I can see the towel on the edge of the sink but it seems miles above me and getting farther, like I'm falling down a well or something. How am I ever going to reach that? I can barely lift my arms now to wipe some of the puke out of my eyes. I put both palms flat on the ground and try to push but I can't even feel the floor so I have no idea how I'm going to do this, I try putting my back against the wall and pushing with my hands and inching up, I slide my feet under me but I slip in some blood that's still making its merry way out of my wrist and I fall back to the tile and smack my head hard off the sink. White spots explode into my vision and I think I throw up again but I'm not sure. Why am I naked?

Oh... I really just want to go to sleep... that would be so much easier I think. I don't want to do this anymore, it's really cold in here and I just want to close my eyes, and I don't mind that my skin is so white because it's really kind of beautiful, delicate sort of like a porcelain doll you know? I'm like a great big hummel... Pete... Mom... I need to get that towel, if I go to sleep I'm not going to wake up, I know it. Okay Jill, let's try again, put your hands on the floor and push, back against the wall and just *move* please for the love of God or you're going to die covered in blood and vomit, Mom and Dad are going to find you naked and soaking in it.

Three

I'm downstairs now, trying to find a coat to put on because I don't think I can get into a full outfit given the state I'm in. I'm barely standing and my skin is so white I think I can see through it, I'm sort of leaning against the walls of my house and pushing myself along like a blind man, stopping every few feet to regain my bearings because it's getting harder and harder to keep my head straight. I think I took my clothes off and got into the bathtub to keep from bleeding on anything important, but I still can't remember. Mom and Dad are out of town, which I think I'm actually grateful for because I wouldn't want them to see me right now and then have to explain what happened. They'd stick me in a hospital somewhere and I'd never get to do anything with my life and I'd wind up chewing my wrists open and drowning myself in the toilet. And I'm not that far gone I don't think, I just got carried away tonight that's all, just a little too upset with myself and now I have to deal with it like a big girl. I must smell terrible, I feel wet all over and I can't tell what's blood and what's puke, but why should it matter if it all came out from inside me, right? The towel is tied firmly around my wrist and I'm making my way to our utility drawer in the kitchen because there's some super glue in there and I think they used that for cuts and stuff a long time ago like in World War One? Ok Jill we have to move away from the wall now, one foot in front of the other, I'm wobbling like I'm on a tightrope but I haven't fallen yet so I think we're doing okay. God, everything is so hazy right now, I think the utility drawer is over by the microwave but that seems so far away.

I make it to the island in the center of our kitchen sort of propping myself up with my arms like a tent, and I can see the drawer over there, it's not too much further. I'm trying to move my feet along but they're barely cooperating which is stupid, c'mon guys we're a team, if I die there'll be no more slippers or massages for you and we can't have *that*. I almost fall, my legs are so shaky, but I'm slowly getting around to the other side of the island. Now the drawer is right in front of me, maybe like five feet, so I throw myself at it but I don't go nearly as far as I need to and my forehead catches the corner of the drawer and I go blind I think because I can't see anything at all.

Four

The darkness peels away really slowly but I can see again. I'm facedown on the floor and I think I crushed my nose. I try to turn my head and there's a noise like crunching gravel and suddenly there's this horrible pain that's so much I can barely register it and I'm pretty sure that means my nose is broken. Shit I've made a hot mess of myself tonight. It's getting really hard to move, like incredibly difficult, but I basically have to do a push up so I don't drag my face across the floor and make myself throw up again. God this is terrible, I don't think I can *do* a push up, I haven't even *tried* one since like eighth grade but I can't move my head unless I do and I need to get into that damn drawer. I draw my hands up until they're on either side of my head and I put my weight into them and try to lift myself at least halfway off the ground, my arm is hurting so bad from the cut but I force it to support me and I manage to twist around and sit on my butt with my back to the drawer. Time to stand now sweetie, let's go, up on your feet. I'm pushing my back against the drawer and trying to get my feet underneath me and it seems to be working, I feel about as sturdy as a milkshake but my legs are lifting me up anyway and suddenly I'm up again and all is right with the world.

I don't remember what I need out of this drawer. *Shit.* I can't go to the hospital, they'd call my parents and then that would be it for me wouldn't it? Breakfast lunch and dinner served through a slot in a door with rubber utensils, and if I'm lucky a mute Native American will smother me with a pillow. Maybe if I call Pete I can go over there and Auger can stitch me up, I don't want to embarrass myself again but I really think I might die if I don't get *someone* to help me, *someone* has to not care that I did this to myself, right? That shouldn't matter if I'm in trouble, should it? God I have no idea where my phone is, or my keys but that's probably best because driving right now would be a silly thing to do but at least my nose isn't bleeding from the fall. Wait it is, nevermind.

Five

Good god, it's such a long walk to their apartment. I'm wearing a coat I found on the couch in the living room but that's all, I didn't even put any shoes on and it's *freezing* and I'm sure I smell like low tide so hopefully no one bothers me. I have no idea what time it is, it's dark outside but there are still people out so I guess maybe like 9? Is it daylight savings yet? I pass by two women carrying bags from a minivan into I guess their house? One of them looks like Mary Tyler Moore if she came out of the womb at age 60 and she gives me a dirty look because she probably thinks I'm a drug addict, which is kind of what I look like right now so I guess I can't be too mad at her but I'm secretly hoping she drops her groceries anyway.

I round the corner more or less on autopilot. I know where I'm going but I can't concentrate on anything so I'm just kind of letting my subconscious take over, feets don't fail me now. Some guy is walking by me now, he looks shady so I do my best to give him a wide berth but my legs feel like oatmeal so instead I almost run into him. He seems confused but I don't offer any explanation and keep walking. I think I hear him behind me going "Hey girl. Hey!" but I don't want to stop or turn around, I don't care what he has to say. If I stop I'm afraid my brain will fry and I won't remember how to get to Pete's, sort of like when you're driving an old car and you have to keep pressing the accelerator while it's idling to keep it from shutting off. Does that make sense? I can't tell.

I'm coming up on the Hardee's that's like seven blocks from my house, so I think I'm making good time although I guess I really have no idea. I can't remember how long I've been out here. I hope they're home. Oh. Oh *shit*, not now, please not now, god*dammit* he's coming up to me…

Auger

One

There's an old man I've noticed around our neighborhood as of late. I see him twice a day out walking a mutt and limping slightly on his left leg. I've thought of approaching him several times, but I'm having trouble determining how to broach the issue. I believe I could help him if I understood the extent of his injury, but in the past I have had some difficult discussions with subjects that I should have been better prepared for. My bedside manner, if anything, will be the downfall of my career.

I've been thinking quite a bit on Pete's question; in point of fact, I spent several hours over the last two days in the library at school re-reading all of our anatomy texts. To my knowledge, he should be able to stab himself in the stomach without causing any serious damage as long as he positions the blade exactly right to avoid piercing his internal organs. To the layperson the injury will seem life-threatening, which is exactly Pete's intention. However, his success in this matter depends almost entirely on the knife he would use. It would be one from The Loaf, of course, but I am ashamed to admit I have never eaten there and have no idea what knives they even have in the building, much less which one Pete would decide to employ. If the blade is too wide or too long or if he stabs himself too deep, the result could be disastrous. He could pierce his stomach or intestines or possibly his kidney, and potentially even his lung if his positioning was far enough off. To reiterate, Pete's idea is not as easy as it sounds.

After the library, I set about going inside The Loaf myself rather than ask Pete about the knives. I wanted to make sure I covered every possible question that might come to mind, which meant I would have to see the instruments for myself. Upon entering the place I was instantly receptive to why Pete seems to hate his job so much; it is the worst type of commercialized headache, impossible to think yet required to react within an instant to whatever ridiculous demands are wrought on you by an over-privileged clientele. Furthermore, they appear wholly incapable of flushing the toilets. I stood in line as patiently as I could manage, ignoring the people around me to our mutual benefit as none of them seemed interested in conversation. When I reached the counter I ordered a bowl of vegetable soup that I had no intention of eating, trying to avoid making any eye contact with the cashier because doing so with strangers has always made me terribly uncomfortable. I don't like it when people look at me.

I approached the pick-up window to collect my food and made a small distraction, a quiet complaint about the temperature of the soup. When the employee turned away to get me a fresh bowl, I took five different knives from his workstation. He gave no indication that he noticed his tools were missing, which added to my understanding of Pete's loathe for the place. "Jake", as this employee's nametag declared him to be, will likely waste the rest of his life in low wage jobs and provide no valuable service to anyone besides reheating my vegetable soup. I made a show of pouring it out into the trashcan as I left.

Two

I saw the old man and his mutt again. I believe I know how I can help him but it will have to wait another day or two. Hopefully his limp worsens, that will make the procedure more challenging.

Pete's problem is actually becoming easier to figure out, provided he uses one of two chef's knives at his disposal, one with a five inch blade and the other with a four. I need to stress to him not to use any of the serrated knives because they have rounded tips and would take a great deal of force to penetrate into his body. Furthermore the serration on the blade would cause excessive and unnecessary tissue damage both externally and internally, leading to his injury no longer merely *appearing* to be critical. He also needs to be careful about positioning the tip against his body; the knife needs to be *thrust*, not pushed, so he will need to bring the blade at least seven to nine inches away from his abdomen before applying the necessary force while keeping his body perfectly still. This leaves a large room for error in an unsteady hand. Indeed, it seems almost too much to entrust to anyone except a surgeon. I should discuss this with him.

Three

I spent more time at the library today, not so much for Pete but because I seem to be getting too concerned with the limping man and his crossbred pet. This happens to me only on the rarest of occasions, when I'm dealing with a subject whose problem, or problems as the case may be, are just beyond my sphere of comprehension. His affected gait could be blamed on any number of things, ranging from arthritis to an old football injury. I hate it when I can't find the answer. I've always detested things like crosswords and logic puzzles and choose your own adventure stories. I don't want to play games, *I want to know.* It crosses the line from challenging to mocking, and I cannot stand being ridiculed. I don't believe any person enjoys it, probably not even the elderly limping gentleman and his dog. Now I've started noticing everything about him, from the time he gets his paper in the morning to the time he comes home from whatever soon-to-be defunct organization had the charity to offer him employment. He never picks up after his mutt.

The library only gave me more questions, which of course was what I was expecting, the one source for the answer lies in the subject himself. Or his doctor. Yes. The subject is an older person, he must have some prescription medication, perhaps even some for the very condition I want to repair. Even if he doesn't discard his old bottles in a typical waste bin, he most likely tosses the receipts and pharmacological information away with everything else. I've already memorized the day and time he takes his garbage to the dumpster out back.

I want to know.

Four

He's late. Perhaps he won't come out tonight, and even if he does there's no guarantee that I will find anything of use in his garbage, but I am still getting frustrated. This happens on occasion as well, when I encounter a subject that is so ungrateful they don't realize what I'm trying to do for them. Every person deserves to be fixed, but it becomes very hard for me when they can't look beyond themselves and see that I deserve this every bit as much as them. My gift is mine but at the same time it belongs to everyone, my great purpose is entirely dependent on others. Even when they insult me like this, I cannot hold back. It wouldn't be fair to anyone, especially not to me.

I am preparing to give up on this tonight when I notice the subject's characteristic limp coming around the corner of the building in the twilight. I draw in a breath quietly and kneel down to avoid being spotted; I have to recover the bag immediately or else I will have no way of knowing which one is his, but if he notices me he will likely become agitated and retreat back to his apartment. I continue to hold my breath as I wait, watching him slowly approach with a plastic refuse bag in hand. With luck it contains exactly what I need to properly diagnose his condition. Finally he reaches the dumpster and with a great effort lobs his bag inside. I might have to check for any signs of weakness in his upper body as well, given this most recent display. My lungs begin to burn slightly, but he is almost halfway to the building now so I release the air from my chest and begin to climb inside the dumpster.

"Hey! Hey… what, what are you doing?!" My full torso is inside the bin right now so I cannot see what the commotion is about. I start to pull myself out when I hear, more urgently, "Are you stuck? Do you need some help?" There are suddenly feeble hands around my waist dragging me backwards and my face catches a jagged edge on the dumpster's sliding door. I can feel myself bleeding, I need to get back to my room immediately and tend to the cut on my face to curtail a myriad of possible infections. The subject is standing before me now, it was he who pulled me out, and he is wearing a concerned expression that quickly dissolves into bewilderment as he notices I am clutching the very bag he just discarded.

"Are… are you stealing my garbage?" he asks me. I offer no response, so he continues. "What are you, like a credit card thief or something? I don't have anything in there but some orange peels and dog food cans, you're wasting your time." I do not respond. He is growing more flustered. "Listen here son, when someone is talking to you, you're supposed to talk back, especially when they've caught you stealing." I remain silent. As I have said, my bedside manner leaves much to be desired. I've never done well in conversation, it makes me uncomfortable and impatient to withdraw. He reaches out to grab the bag from me but I step back quickly. "Now dammit, I'm being reasonable! Who the hell are you? Do you live here? Do you want me to call the police?" What a ridiculous question. What a foolish thing. He reaches out again, this time to grab me, and I am so distracted by his sudden effort that I make no attempt to dodge him and his hands close firmly around my midsection, and a look plays across his face that tells me he instantly regrets this decision.

I should explain very quickly that I wear my tools in an oversized leather wrap beneath my clothes every time I leave the apartment. I do this because of a time I found a young boy, perhaps ten years old, laying in a ditch with his head crushed against a stone after having fallen from his bicycle. I might have been able to help him had I been carrying some of my instruments; at the very least I could have released some of the pressure in his skull and made his death less painful. Since then I have learned my lesson. So this subject, the limping man, has just grabbed my leather wrap and he doesn't understand what he is touching. He says, "Oh my God, are you wearing ladies' underwear?" and he recoils in horror.

"Your leg is hurt," I say to him. "I've seen you limping. I can help you." He backs away from me though, and I can tell he is going to call our landlord and probably the police as well. "What are you talking about? Are you helping me by stealing my garbage? I go to a *doctor* for my leg, not some dumpster diving freak in women's underwear! Stay away from me!" I reach into my pocket for my pin, forgetting that it hasn't been there in many years. I do this occasionally, when people look at me. The blood on my face feels hot. I can smell it. I need to get back inside and treat the wound. This subject is clearly lost to me for now. I start to walk towards him with every intention of simply passing him by and returning to our apartment, but he seems to regard this as a threat and panics.

He has drawn a gun. This is unsurprising, as many older people in our neighborhood are vocal Second Amendment supporters, but is no less troublesome. I don't feel he is in the correct frame of mind to be wielding a firearm. "Just stay where you are, okay? Just stay still!" he says to me. I continue to advance, but slowly, deliberately trying to move around him. Hopefully this will diffuse the situation. "I said don't move!" he almost wails. "Stop, okay! Please stop!" and he makes eye contact with me despite my efforts to avoid this. I freeze. I have no desire to speak to him at all, yet I feel like there is something I can say to calm him. I look down, away from him. Sometimes this helps, I have difficulty thinking when people look at me. "I want to know," I say at last. This is the best explanation I can offer, but he hasn't lowered his weapon. In fact, he seems more upset by what I've said. "Son, just... just don't move, okay?" He moves backward towards his building, still pointing the gun and not taking his eyes off of me. I hate it when people stare. There is nothing remarkable about what I am doing, why is he acting this way? If he's nervous about the trash, I can leave it here and return to collect it later. Maybe that will help the situation. I drop the bag and take a step.

He shoots me. The bullet hits in the lower abdomen, I feel it strike the leather and my surgical saw beneath. I hope it isn't broken but judging by the injury I suddenly feel, the saw must certainly be destroyed. I try again to find the words to explain to the subject that I am no threat to him, though I still will not look him in the eyes because I don't want to make things more difficult than they have already become. I can't seem to think right now, I reach into my pocket again for my pin but it isn't there and hasn't been for some time and will continue to not be for some time to come. I do this when I start to feel upset. "You should put the gun away." I unzip my jacket to inspect the damage, displaying numerous rows of metal instruments, and as I remove my saw I am saddened to see that it is indeed ruined.

I'm shot again, this time a surface wound in my upper right bicep which causes me to lose my grip on the broken saw. It isn't a serious injury, but I need to get inside right away. I look the subject in the face, but at the bridge of his nose instead of in the eyes.

"I need to get inside now," I say. He is in a state of shock, I can tell. This could work to my advantage. He says, "I didn't... now son, just sit your ass down and we'll call... who the hell are you?" The gun wavers. An instant later I have detached his spinal cord and he is dead, and I am dragging his body back to the dumpster, albeit with some difficulty considering the damage to my right arm. I just wanted to know. People can ruin so many things without ever realizing. It makes my head hurt sometimes.

Five

The gunshot to my body is more serious than I initially thought. I became too weak and nearly collapsed trying to hide the old man inside the dumpster. He needs to be properly disposed of like any other subject, but I will have to return to him later tonight once I've been able to repair myself. I'm in my room now, and under the blue lights I can see that a shard of metal from the surgical saw has been forced into my midsection. It has carved a line into my belly button, a jagged ridge extending an inch to my left. The bullet itself did not make it inside, which is a small relief but still leaves a moderate amount of damage to contend with. My shoulder is comparatively fine, only a few stitches will be necessary to fix the injury.

I'm sitting on the operating table, swabbing away blood from my body as I spread the wound open to retrieve the metal. I rarely use anesthesia when I operate for several reasons, the foremost being that it is very expensive and impossibly difficult to come by. In addition, when I am working on a subject I feel that it detracts from the challenge of the procedure to have them drugged and unresponsive, except in extreme circumstances. In those instances I do have some low-level general anesthesia to prevent subjects from thrashing around and hurting themselves, but I never use localized. It spoils everything. In cases such as tonight when I have to work on myself, anesthesia would be foolish.

The metal shard does not appear to have lodged itself terribly deep inside of me, which allows me to rule out the possibility of any serious internal injuries. Also, I would probably feel a near-paralyzing agony in my torso if a vital organ had been damaged. Since I do not feel this type of pain, I reason there are no internal complications that require any attention. I extract the metal with some forceps and a steady hand while applying light pressure with a wad of gauze in case I start to bleed profusely. As soon as the shard is out of my body I cover the wound with the gauze and apply enormous pressure. Now I'm standing from the operating table and moving to my tools to retrieve a needle and some catgut to suture it closed.

I should explain that physical pain has always been an alien sensation to me. It strikes me as more of a curiosity than anything else. I have been seriously injured on numerous occasions, but I have never felt crippled or dull of focus. In point of fact, I usually do not notice any damage to my person unless it is to some degree of severity. Even if I am bleeding, I rarely react before my clothing is completely stained. I smell blood, true, but the drawback is that I *always* smell blood, so that particular sense can only be trusted under extreme circumstances. Pain is irritating, but never distracting. I need a new saw.

Both wounds are now closed and bandaged. I put on a new shirt and carry the bullet torn bloodrag I was wearing earlier down to the dumpster with me. I climb inside with my old saw, a backup in case of emergencies. Two of its teeth have been broken off, but I sharpen the remaining ones with some regularity. Besides, this particular procedure does not call for elegance. I carry the bundles to Pete's car, wrapped in bags I find in the dumpster, and drive off to dispose of them. I will be unable to cast as wide a net tonight, because daylight is rapidly approaching and I believe Pete has work in the morning. He will notice if his car is gone. I may not even have enough time to clean it, which could cause a conflict. He is unlikely to suspect that I borrowed his car, and if he has a long enough shift I can take it from The Loaf to get cleaned and return it before he clocks out for the day, but I would rather not take that chance. One of his co-workers may notice me taking his car, or he may decide to drive to another restaurant on his lunch break, which varies every day he works so there is no way for me to coordinate around it. There are too many uncontrollable factors.

It would be better if Pete didn't go in to work. Yes. There is no other way to avoid it. I'm confident in his procedure now, so perhaps tomorrow morning is the time to discuss it with him. I look at the old man's garbage bag in the seat next to me and decide. I wanted to know. Pete wants to know. I'm going to tell him I have solved his problem, because Jill said that's what friends are for and I think I'm finally beginning to understand what that means.

Hardee's

It is eleven thirty P.M. The restaurant hasn't been open for hours, but there are still a few cars in the parking lot belonging to the remaining employees inside finishing their closing duties. Two teenage boys are skateboarding in a far corner of the lot, trying repeatedly to ollie off of the curb but reaching no success as of yet.

A patrol car cruises slowly into a space near the front of the building. The policeman at the wheel has a nametag that says "Owens" and he nods a salute to one of the Hardee's employees he recognizes from repeated visits to the drive thru for complimentary sodas. The employee nods back and resumes mopping the entryway, wishing he was at home playing *Gears of War* with a bottle of Steel Reserve.

Owens notices the boys at the far end of the lot and steps out of his car. They finally spot him as he is approaching and let out matching groans to express their disappointment.

"Pack it up guys, you know better." Owens has dealt with them several times before and can almost remember their names, though not clearly enough to try and use them.

"Come on man!" one of the boys complains. "Where are we supposed to go?"

His partner contributes: "Yea, shouldn't you be glad we're not doing drugs or killing people?"

"I am *thrilled* you're not doing drugs or killing people," Owens says, "because we would be having a very different conversation. Rules is rules, and you both know what they are."

The boys make a dramatic show of their exasperation, deliberately trying to linger in hopes that Owens might relent. He does not. "Don't make me take the boards. Aren't there curbs in front of your houses you can break your teeth on?" They concede, the battle lost. As they turn to leave the lot, one of them stops, staring at something behind Owens. "Holy shit." He slowly raises one hand and points.

"Are you kidding?" Owens says. "Do I look like Elmer Fudd? Pack up your shit and get going before I forget what a nice guy I am."

"Officer Owens, I'm serious," the boy says. "There's a fucked up white girl behind you." Owens turns and sees that the boy isn't lying. A small girl, maybe early twenties, is staggering by the lot. She is clad in a brown overcoat but her legs and feet are bare. Her skin is sickeningly white like a ghost, her eyes are hollow sunken cavities above a swollen purple nose and her black hair is matted down in streaks with some kind of reddish-yellow paste that's also staining her face. Owens thinks she looks like a zombie.

"Man, that lady's on *crack*," the other kid says.

"Go home." Owens starts to walk towards the girl. He looks back at the skateboarders and sees they have not moved. "Leave now or I'm going to impound your shit and burn it!"

"Okay okay!" The teenagers get on their boards and ride away. Owens mutters to himself and returns his attention to the girl. She very well might be on crack or meth or something similar. She may be a prostitute. Whatever the case, she appears strung out, unable to walk in a straight line and seemingly lacking any real strength in her movements. She's clearly in some kind of distress. As he gets closer, Owens detects an odor he has only experienced twice before; this girl smells like death. By now she has spotted him and Owens can tell she has no interest in speaking to him. He thinks to himself *well it's too late for that, honey*.

"Good evening ma'am," he says. The girl stops and after several moments finally croaks, "Hi."

"Do you have any kind of identification on you?" Owens asks, fairly certain he already knows the answer. She shakes her head no. "Ok, well what's your name? Do you live around here?"

"Jill," she says. "Jillian Archer Edison. I live around the corner. Back there." She tries to gesture, almost stumbles but then recovers and withdraws back into herself, rocking back and forth slightly like she's on the deck of a ship. Owens writes her name down, then asks for her address and copies that down as well. "What's your date of birth, Jill?" She tells him August 5th, 1988, which he also records. "Can you tell me what you're doing walking around here all by yourself so late at night? I'd hate to see something happen to you. Plus you aren't wearing much and it's a bit cold outside. Are you in some kind of trouble? Is everything alright?"

Jill offers no immediate response. Finally: "I'm just walking to a friend's house."

"And who's your friend? Where does your friend live?" Owens is well aware that something has happened to this girl that she is unwilling to discuss with him, so he thinks he will try to piece some kind of picture together without her picking up on it. "Just a friend," she says. "He's not far." Her pupils aren't dilated, her breath stinks but not like alcohol. She looks like she was beaten, and Owens decides that the physical evidence of the assault must be beneath the conspicuous jacket she is currently wearing. "Jill, there are some things about your appearance that are worrying me," he says.

Jill says nothing. "Is that blood in your hair and on your face?" Owens asks. "No," Jill says immediately. "I threw up."

"Why did you throw up? Are you sick?"

"Yes I'm sick," Jill says, starting to walk away. "I'm really sick, and my friend is going to help me."

Shit, Owens thinks. "Well are you sure you want to walk all the way there? I'd be happy to give you a ride."

"No thank you," she says. "I'll be fine. Good night." She staggers away, dragging herself down the sidewalk towards the main road.

     Owens curses to himself. Preferring not to see Jill dead on the morning news, he checks the information she provided on his computer. She lives in a big house a few blocks from the Hardee's, much too nice for someone her age to be living in even with roommates. It must be her parents' house, Owens reasons, and he considers driving by to see if anyone is home. He sighs, "Cover your ass", and decides that a quick look at the house and an incident report wouldn't be unreasonable. He currently has nothing else to do anyway.

Pete

One

     I'm dreaming I'm floating in a big water tank at Sea World. It's a bright, beautiful sunny day and Fozzie Bear and Scooter from *Muppet Babies* are standing on a platform above me, giving me instructions on how to swim. But the thing is, even though I should be totally at ease with the two of them as my coaches, I can tell that there is a *shark* in here with me. I just know it, I can't explain how. Sometimes that happens in dreams, I'm sure you've experienced it. At any rate, I'm trying to argue with them that perhaps now is not the best time for me to be learning the butterfly stroke, but they don't seem to hear. Maybe the Olympic trials are coming up.

     So I'm treading water and I can *feel* the shark circling beneath me, but Fozzie starts in with his Waka Waka routine and no human being can resist *that*, so now I'm laughing along with him despite the rising terror that grips me. After another second or two I feel the thing tear into my leg and I shout "Fuck you Fozzie!" which is something I never thought I would say, dream or otherwise.

Two

     I wake up in my room, wearing sweatpants and nothing else. The area of my body normally covered by a shirt is currently wrapped in a sizeable bandage, and when I try to move I feel a tremendous pain in my abdomen. I'm confused at first, trying to remember what happened and why. Or maybe I'm still dreaming, it's pretty unclear at this point. Funny how I can be in an obviously serious situation and be unable to retrace the steps that led me there. I swing my legs around, clenching my teeth through it all, and make a Herculean effort to stand up. I stumble at first but I fight off the pain and get to my feet in spite of it. Good god, I never thought just trying to get out of bed would kick my ass so much unless I'd had a *real* good time the night before. Judging by the mummy wraps I'm currently sporting, I must've had a blast.

I shuffle over to my closet and grab a hooded sweatshirt from inside, which I throw over myself and zip up. I don't feel like trying to pull a t-shirt on over the bandage, and I *really* don't feel like trying to take the bandage off. It could be a festering boil or Kuato from *Total Recall*, or worse yet it could be a tribal tattoo. I walk out to the kitchen, past Auger's room and the common room, because I feel like I haven't eaten in days. I spot my cereal bowl from the other morning before work still sitting in the sink, rinsed but unwashed, and then I turn and see Auger standing in the doorway.

"Uh, hey Auger," I stammer, rattled a bit by his sudden appearance.

"How are you feeling?" he asks, looking at me but not really. He never *really looks* at anyone, I've noticed. He either picks a spot on your face or one just past it on the wall behind you and focuses on that.

"Ah, fine, I guess." I unzip my sweatshirt and gesture to the bandage beneath. "Do you know what happened here?" Auger seems confused that I should ask. "You don't remember?" he says. "That's what you wanted. I figured it out for you."

There is something alien in this statement that gives me pause, because it sounds like Auger is searching for approval and I would sooner expect him to sing the theme from *Ghostbusters*. Then I see a chef's knife from The Loaf resting in the drying rack next to the sink and I remember everything.

It's funny how things happen in slow motion when you've experienced a major system shock. I feel my hands drop to my sides for what seems like an eternity, I'm watching them fall and I'm thinking *Jesus this is taking a long time*, I look at Auger and he's still somewhat bewildered as if nothing in the world is making sense right now, and I can't really blame him because that's exactly the way I am feeling. *He stabbed me. He stuck a knife in me and let me bleed out on the floor.* I turn to the sink to look for something, *anything* I can use to defend myself and I settle on the chef's knife from work, the very instrument Auger scrubbed and rinsed and left in the drying rack after pulling it from my body. I shoot my hand out, feel my fingers close around the handle and draw it in to wield against my roommate, waving it in front of me with what I hope is some measure of menace. Auger doesn't react to it at all, he still is just standing in the doorway and staring at me but not *really* at me, his features twisted only slightly in an effort to process his incredulity.

"Pete," he says. "You asked me to help you and I helped you."

"Help me?!" I shout, and I tug at my bandaged torso with my free hand. "You call this *help*? Auger, you could've *killed* me! What were you thinking?"

Auger looks away and says nothing. He's wrestling with something, some kind of weird barking in his mind, I don't know. But there's a problem up there, I've always known it but I guess I've just been ignoring it subconsciously. Or maybe it was consciously. Auger scares the shit out of me and right now I've never been more scared in my life. I can't think of anything else to do except stand right here with this knife until he goes back into his room and then I have to get the hell out. I can go to Nick's or to Jill's, her parents like me and they won't mind me staying if I explain that my roommate is a lunatic and he stabbed me in the stomach...

Oh no.

Auger looks at me, *really* at me this time and I can tell it's tearing him apart to do so even for a second. "I..." he struggles, then mercifully he pulls his eyes away and disappears. I hear the door to his room open and close, but I can't move for several moments. I'm just standing in the kitchen, bandaged up and holding this knife in a hand that's shaking like a leaf on a tree and I realize this is all my fault. I drop the cutlery, sending it clattering to the tile below, and I pull the wrap away from my midsection to see a stitched wound in my stomach, right about where it would need to be for me to get sent home from work with a large cash settlement.

Three

I park my car in a space no less than seventy miles from the entrance to The Loaf and make my way inside, nodding to familiar coworkers as I cross the restaurant towards the managers' office in the back. I tap on the door's narrow glass inlay and wait for someone to open up. Todd answers. In addition to being the assistant manager, he is also an insufferable dick, so this conversation is going to be a whole lot of fun.

"Where were you yesterday?" he demands immediately. "No call, no show is grounds for a disciplinary review, you know. You're a trainer, you *should* know that."

"Yea, sorry Todd," I say. "I actually got hurt kind of bad yesterday and wasn't able to make any calls." I unzip my jacket and show him the bandage. He studies it for a moment, sweat glistening on his balding head. Todd sort of looks like a bull terrier, if bull terriers could grow goatees. He is about a foot shorter than me, so I'm getting an excellent view of the aforementioned sweat beading up on his cranium.

"Open that up please," he says, gesturing to the bandage. You've got to be kidding me.

"You've got to be kidding," I say.

"No," Todd says, looking up at me. "No, I'm not kidding at all. Like I said, no call no show is a fire-able offense. So open it up."

I sigh heavily to illustrate how totally ridiculous this is. Maybe I should stab *him* instead, not a jury in the world would convict me. I unwrap the bandage enough to make the wound visible and display it for him to examine. Doubtless he will be drawing on every bit of his experience watching *House* to determine the legitimacy of my injury. Todd stares at it for several seconds, rubbing his chin between his thumb and forefinger like he's appraising furniture.

"What did you do, exactly?" he asks finally, with the same tone my parents would use to find out how I broke the vase. So I start in with my rehearsed explanation: "I was helping my friend move some stuff and we dropped a picture frame and some of the glass went into my stomach. I spent the night in the emergency room."

"Hmm," Todd mumbles, considering this. "Why didn't your friend call to let us know?" This is a bullshit question, because it clearly says in our Employee Handbook that no one else but you can call The Loaf to try and excuse an absence. I tell Todd this, and add, "As a manager, you *should* know that." He gives me a look that says he wishes he were more intimidating and turns to the schedule hanging on the inside of the door.

"When do you work again?" he asks, despite having the schedule clearly in front of him. "Tomorrow," I answer. "And then the next two days after that."

"No, just tomorrow," Todd says, crossing my name off for the rest of the week. "I think you need a little extra time to recover from your injury."

"But not tomorrow, which is precisely one day after I hurt myself?"

Todd shoots another glare and then crosses me off for tomorrow as well. "Have it your way. I'll see you next Monday."

Dammit. I really don't want to miss any work until *after* I stab myself. "Thanks for understanding, Todd." I walk back up front and get Jake to put some soup and sandwiches in a bag for me, because fuck Todd. I walk out to the car and climb back inside, handing the bag to Auger in the passenger seat. "Is there any way I can chop Todd's head off and have it seem like an accident?" I ask him.

Auger blinks. "No."

Nuts.

Jill

One

I made it past the cop, that's good, I think he was close to making me go with him to the hospital or something but I got out of there just in time. Now I'm making my way down the main street, I can't remember exactly how long it's been since the parking lot but I feel like maybe ten minutes? This is so weird, it's like that game you play in the pool where you let all the air out of your lungs so you can sink to the bottom and sit. I used to do that all the time when I was little and pretend I had a table and chairs down there and it was like a tea party. That's how I feel right now, that underwater feeling, weight and weightlessness at the same time. I pass a bunch of bright neon signs, an auto dealership and maybe a Starbucks I think and some song lyric passes through my brain, *one great big festering neon distraction*, but I can't turn the gears enough right now to remember what the song even *is* so I stop thinking about it and just let it repeat over and over in my mind like a scratched up CD that won't stop skipping.

God, it really is a long way to their apartment, I didn't realize. It's getting so hard to move, I look down at my arms and my bare legs and I'm so *white* it scares me. I should be dead, I must be dying right now. I've never felt this scatterbrained in my life, like a girl on *The Hills*. I'd always hoped when the end came I'd be pretty lucid, I'd be able to unleash some last words that would just echo through time with wisdom and insight and just *value*, you know? Like seeing the light at the end of the tunnel would bring out the most amazing thing I'd been holding inside me for so long. Right now I don't see a tunnel, it's actually getting kind of hard to see at all, I can't focus and I'm laboring under that constant head-rush feeling when all the blood shoots out of your brain after you stand up too fast. Maybe that means I'm not dying. That would be nice.

There's this loud noise at the edge of my hearing that's been going on for a little while now, and all of a sudden I can make it out against everything that's sloshing around in my brain. It's a horn, like someone is leaning on their horn and it's so *loud* it must be right *next* to me so I stop walking and as I do I feel myself fall straight down to the sidewalk on my butt. I hear a car door open and some footsteps against the passing traffic and there's two legs next to me now carrying with them a smell of bad air freshener, those horrible pine tree things you see in cabs and shuttle buses. Some rocks on the pavement are poking me and I remember that I'm totally naked underneath this jacket so I try to draw my feet in some but I can hardly move so I stop.

"Hey are you okay?" A man's voice from somewhere above the legs. "Is there someone you want me to call?" I mumble a response, but I have no idea what it is. I feel myself being lifted to my feet, a breeze in my lady parts tells me my coat is open at the bottom and a sharp intake of breath in my ear tells me the mystery man sees it too. Ugh. I don't need this right now, not another Jake. I'm loaded into the backseat of a car, vinyl seats in pretty bad shape and that crucial air freshener smell. A taxi, like I thought. The door shuts behind me and I hear the guy climb into the driver's seat and put the car in gear. "Where are you headed? Pretty girl like you shouldn't be out alone this time of night. Let me take you someplace, okay?"

I don't say anything, I'm still struggling to get my bearings. Getting tossed into a car sort of shook me all up, like when you drop your pencil box and everything inside is all Hurricane Katrina. Suddenly I can feel him closer, stale breath on my cheek as I lay across the back seat, and he says "You on something? You need a fix? I can help." I say "No" into the vinyl and work myself into a normal sitting position. I see him now, an older guy with maybe thirteen teeth and a package of Skoal in his breast pocket, long gray hair slithering out from underneath an old watch cap. He looks like he belongs in another century, like he hitched a ride with Bill and Ted. He's staring at me expectantly, the car is in drive but we haven't moved. "No," I repeat, and I tell him Pete's address and ask him to take me there. He thinks about it for a second then says "You work, girl? Are you working?" and I assume he's asking because he wants to know if I can pay him so

58

I say yes, I'm working, and he smiles broadly and says "Okay-hay" with a laugh and we drive off.

Two

I'm drifting in and out now, I'm not sure what day it is anymore or how long I've been like this. I can't even remember when I cut myself, it seems forever ago like I was *born* a zombie just staggering on the brink. At one point I notice the driver has angled his mirror so he can see between my legs so I fold my hands together and put them in my lap to block his view. He grunts to himself and I slip off again.

I open my eyes and see that I'm lying across the seat, looking up out of the window at the tops of some brick buildings that I think I might recognize but don't all bricks look the same? You're just being silly Jilly, you could be anywhere right now and not know the difference. The car has stopped and my door opens and I feel rough hands on my legs pulling me outside. He gets a cheap feel like I expect him to and props me up against the cab, sort of shakes me a bit and says "Hey girl, crazy girl are we here? Is this the place?" and he turns my head around for me so hard he's wrenching my neck but I'm not really feeling any pain right now anyway. These buildings *are* familiar I think, where was it I wanted to go? I mumble something and he lets go of me, I slide down to the ground and sit still against the car. He says "Crazy bitch" to I guess himself because no one else is listening and I hear him moving around to the other side of the car. Suddenly the door opens up right next to my head and his arms come through and hook under my shoulders and he drags me back inside, across the vinyl seat again. His pants are undone and I think to myself *here it comes* and sure enough he tears my jacket open and starts trying to do his thing and I'm actually kind of laughing inside, this is so *ridiculous* to me, this guy has no idea how bad his night is about to get, I've got just enough strength left in me to make sure and I still don't see a light or a tunnel at all but I'm pretty sure I'll be dead by morning so why not? I moan and he takes the bait, and everything seems so funny to me I just can't believe I'm about to die.

Incident

The cab sits in the parking lot of the apartment complex, idling by the mailboxes with both rear doors standing open like yellow wings. It rocks slightly, commotion bubbling inside until it finally spills out into the night beyond. The driver falls out onto his back, pants unfastened, his breath coming out in spasms as blood gushes from his groin in torrents. Jill slides out of the opposite side onto her knees, completely nude and doubled over, laughing uncontrollably as she spits gore from her mouth. She reaches into the car and closes her hand around her jacket as she lets herself fall backward to lie on the pavement, pulling the jacket out and over her like a blanket, still laughing so hard she thinks her ribs may crack.

The driver's breathing lapses into wheezing groans of agony. He tries to crawl around the cab to Jill, moving very slowly across the pavement. "I'm going to kill you bitch!" he sputters. Jill laughs, tears in her eyes, then turns her head and spits out another chunk of her attacker's ruined testicle. "It's totally worth it," she says, laughing again. Oh this is so funny, so *funny*, she thinks to herself. Much better than drowning in puke on the bathroom floor. *Lifetime* might even make a movie about me, that would be *hilarious*.

None of the residents have come outside to investigate, though a few lights have clicked on and several blinds have been peeked through. They've heard this type of ruckus before and long ago decided never to get involved, always better to just sit inside and call the police to take care of it. Except one door *does* open, and someone *does* come outside, a pale young man with black hair hanging in front of an expressionless face. He moves quickly to Jill, not walking so much as *gliding*, and lifts her up off of the ground, carrying her away to the door he came from and setting her inside. He turns back to the cab. The driver has struggled to his feet and now leans against the trunk of his car, sucking in air and cursing it back out. He sees Auger and starts to speak, but Auger's hands flick out like a whip and suddenly the driver finds he can say nothing at all. He tries but can only gurgle, he feels his tongue hanging limp and can almost feel a *breeze* on it. He looks down and sees his jaw on the ground between his feet, collecting blood like a rain barrel as it pours from his face, and he is gripped with real horror now for the first and last time in his life. Auger's hands dart several more times, each motion a broad artist's stroke reducing the man before him into a quivering hunk of meat, each strike delivering a massive and ultimately fatal injury. The driver tries to lift his hands in a feeble defense but finds the tendons severed, his arms hanging uselessly like rags on a clothesline. He gets a final glimpse of glinting metal before his eyes are cut from their sockets. Auger allows the driver to crumble onto the ground before pulling a rib spreader from his leather wrap, pressing it into the driver's exposed sternum and splitting it with a crack like dried wood. The man is dead but Auger is not finished, his hands bore in and remove pieces like apples at a farmer's market. He is not out to learn anything this time. He is a force of nature and he will have all the blood he wants.

The door behind Auger starts to open then quickly swings shut again. Inside, Pete steps slowly back, cradling Jill like a new bride but not looking away from his roommate, the horrible black specter, the ghost and his steel punishment.

Pete

One

With the next couple of days off from work, and with me not going to classes anymore, I have a lot of time to construct my ultimate stabbing plan. Auger says it's best to wait a few weeks to give me time to heal up a bit before inflicting another injury, and I'm pretty sure I agree with him, so that gives me even more time to think. Probably the most important thing I have to consider is that in order for me to get a settlement of any substance I have to be injured in a manner that demonstrates management's failure to provide a safe working environment for me. This is not as easy as it sounds. As I outlined earlier, slipping onto a knife won't work, and I doubt I can convince anybody to stick me while I'm on the clock, not even Jill. She'd probably flip out if she knew I was serious about it.

Auger wrote out detailed instructions for me, like where to position the blade and how much force to use, that sort of thing. And he keeps stressing that I have to remain perfectly still when it happens or else I'll be in serious trouble, which I guess makes sense. That rattles me a bit because I've never had the steadiest hands in the world, although I am a force to be reckoned with at *Trauma Center: Second Opinion* on the Nintendo Wii. Tangent: it's hilarious to watch Auger play this game. I really recommend it if you're ever on our side of town, it's like watching a monkey try to use an ATM. He never appears outwardly frustrated, but one time during a particularly difficult stitching section, he dropped the remote, got an orange from the kitchen and sutured it flawlessly, then set it on the table and went into his room for the rest of the night. Fantastic.

Two

Am I losing my way again? I can never tell when it's happening, which is probably a good indicator that it is. I'm so wrapped up in this idea of hurting myself for money that I just don't *do* anything anymore. School got boring again, nothing new there, but I haven't been doing any writing or painting or even any *reading*. What am I even here for if I can't bring myself to do the things that I enjoy? What do I want to be? Where do I want my life to go? I have no idea. But the answer isn't what's starting to scare me; I don't even ask the *question* anymore, and that's what's truly terrifying. I don't think Auger has been going to classes either. Maybe his social withdrawl has gotten so bad he can't manage it. Am *I* drowning with *him* or is *he* drowning with *me*? Or am I reading too much into my life, the life of a shiftless twenty-something who thinks the world owes him big time?

I saw Nick for the first time in a few weeks the other day for coffee, and he's almost *begging* me to pack up and leave now. This is weird, because you have to understand Nick is exactly like me except with less ambition. He works at Blockbuster Video; that's all he does and that's all he's ever wanted to do. There isn't a creative bone or a single spark of imagination in his body. But he's my friend and he's always looked out for me, and he has a bad habit of being right about things. Maybe I do need to get out. Maybe I can take my huge cash settlement and just beat the dust of this place off my heels, go someplace nice for a while and see what happens. A change of scenery might help change my perspective, Nick said. I asked him how my perspective could change if I don't seem to have any. That shut him up a little harsher than I meant, but he still paid for the coffee.

Three

We get back from my visit with Todd at The Loaf and Auger disappears into his room almost immediately. It seems ridiculous that I should feel guilty about him stabbing me, but I still do. I get so damn drunk all the time I can't remember half the conversations I have. People must think I'm crazy, when I repeat things to them I said while I was blacking out or when I stare at them blankly at the mention of some deep moment we shared while I was too intoxicated to remember. This is probably why I have about four friends in the entire world, and one of them locks himself in his room all the time.

Is Auger my friend? I really don't know. He's just kind of *there*; sort of like the pet hamster I got as a kid, I can never really decide how I feel about him. Though I must admit I haven't been able to completely shake the fear I felt standing there in the kitchen, guilt notwithstanding. Like I said, I saw something inside Auger that I kept pretending wasn't there, and it's gotten harder to ignore ever since.

I need to get out of here, definitely. I hate my job and I'm not going to school anymore anyway, so what's holding me back? Yeah, I know. Jill. I think she'd go with me, if I asked. She just packed up and left right after high school without a second thought and she's always talking about how she wants to take off for good this time, never come back. That's what I need, absolutely that's what I need. I'm going to ask her. It doesn't have to be weird, it's not a boyfriend/girlfriend thing, at least not yet. We can just be roommates like Auger and I, and as far as I know I've never been on a date with Auger, unless he's doing more than just bandaging me while I'm passed out. I can call Jill now, I know she's not at work today, I'll just call her and invite myself over and we'll talk about it. She'll say yes, I *know* she will. I need some new influences in my life besides Auger, someone that doesn't speak in cryptic monosyllables and look like *The Nightmare Before Christmas* 365 days a year. I need Jill.

Although, she *does* look like *The Nightmare Before Christmas*.

Four

Five minutes maybe, that's all. Simultaneously the longest and shortest of my whole life.

It's almost one in the morning, I've been trying to call Jill since about eight and she isn't answering. I'm worried so I keep calling, she never takes this long to get back to me, no matter what's going on and I know she's alone this weekend because her parents are gone and I can't stop thinking about the other night with the scars on her wrists so I'm fretting like a mother hen, I can't help it. I'm trying again, Auger is standing with me in the common room as I pace around listening to the ring on the other end and then her voicemail for what must be the twentieth time that night. I curse and snap my phone shut, stuffing it back into my pocket. I want to be drinking so bad right now but I know I shouldn't, if Jill is in some kind of trouble I want to be able to help her and I can't do that if I'm passed out in my apartment. Auger is both motionless and expressionless, just watching me like a toddler watching his dad cuss out the electric company over the phone. He's been out here with me all night but he hasn't said anything since asking me what was going on, and that was almost four hours ago.

Maybe it's nothing, maybe she just dropped her phone in the toilet or something and she doesn't remember my number so she can't call me on her house line. But she has my number memorized, doesn't she? I know hers by heart. I'm pacing back and forth, looking at everything and nothing at the same time because all I'm really seeing is Jill, maybe hurt and maybe not. I hear a car pull up and idle just outside our building. A door opens and shuts, probably a cab spilling out some kids too drunk to drive home, which is what I *want* to be right now but I can't. I've let her down in the past like that. There have been nights where I'm way too bombed to see straight and she'll call me really late and I won't be able to answer the phone, and the next morning I'll find a teary message in my voicemail because she was having trouble and she *needed* my help and I couldn't be there for her. I don't want to do that anymore, in this moment I've decided I'm never going to make myself useless again. That's all I've done since I got kicked out of high school and it's time to stop before I waste my whole life and everyone around me.

A man shouts, right outside our door. I look over at Auger but he's already gone, already moving towards the entryway to see outside. I follow him.

Sure enough, there's a yellow taxi in the parking lot, maybe forty yards from our apartment. Both of its rear doors are open, and on the side facing us there is a naked girl lying on the pavement with a jacket draped across her, laughing hysterically. I see a man that looks like a cancer-ridden version of Brian Johnson from AC/DC crawl alongside the rear of the vehicle. His pants are undone, but there's a copious amount of crimson liquid shielding his bait and tackle from view. I suck in a breath as I realize his groin is soaked in blood.

"Auger," I start, but when I turn to him I see that he's gone. I look back outside, trying to decide what to do. The girl has blood all over her face, she looks like a zombie. The guy is rounding the car now, hissing something that I can't hear but I know isn't anything positive. She looks like a china doll, laying there and laughing her head off. I reach for my phone because all I can think of right now is dialing 911, but suddenly something occurs to me and I stop.

She looks like Jill.

*She **is** Jill.*

The phone falls from my hand and shatters on the ground. I hear it crunch under Auger's feet as he sweeps past me, through the door and outside to the idling taxi. I'm frozen in place, I can't believe that's *Jill*, she has blood all over her. Oh god, Jill, what happened? Auger scoops her up effortlessly, for such a small guy he really seems to have a surprising amount of power. He brings her back inside and sets her down in our entryway, right at my feet, and immediately I feel the gears start turning again. I bend down and slide my arms gently underneath her, good god she is so *white* it makes me sick to my stomach. She smells like Satan's underwear but I don't care at all, instinctively I lean in and kiss her head and then her face and hold her close. Fuck me, *what do I do?* What happened to you Jill? I keep asking her over and over but she's out, maybe for good. "Auger," I say. "Auger, help me!" He doesn't respond, and when I pull my head away from Jill to look for him I freeze all over again.

Auger is back outside, standing in front of the cab and the creepy looking guy with the bloody pants, but his arms are flying crazily around like a psychotic orchestra conductor, a black shadow flickering like fading candlelight. He's taking pieces off of the guy at an alarming rate, little chunks like dog food that keep wetly smacking the pavement. Auger moves to the side slightly and I can see the man doesn't even have a *face* anymore, the bottom half is totally gone and his tongue is dangling like a curtain rope. He's being cut apart and he can't even defend himself, he just shudders to the ground and endures every strike Auger delivers. Auger stops and I see him pull this thing out of his coat that looks like a miniature lumberjack saw, a long dual handled blade that curves upwards and glints in the streetlight like a toothy disembodied smile that makes me think of the Cheshire cat. He brings it down with a meaty thump, grips the two handles tightly and pushes it forward like he's shaving ice for a sculpture. There's a sickening crack, then a sound like rushing water. Auger puts the saw away and lurches his arms forward, literally reaching inside the man's body and *tearing things out*.

I gag and almost drop Jill on the floor. She groans slightly, her eyes flutter a bit but she doesn't quite come out of it. I back slowly away from the door, not taking my eyes off Auger and wondering whether or not I should barricade the damn thing to keep him from coming back inside. Instead I decide to put Jill in my bed and clean her up with a washcloth and a bowl of hot water. I'm not thinking about Auger at all anymore, I don't care what he's doing out there. I kiss her again, her face tastes like blood and bile but I don't mind much. She has a towel tied to her wrist. I don't need to undo it to know what's underneath. I love you Jill, please don't die.

Five

The front door closes and I snap awake. I've been passed out with my head on Jill's chest for maybe ten minutes. She's still breathing but she looks terrible, like a bloody puke-stained ghost. I can hear Auger moving around in the kitchen, hear him drop the lid shut on the chest freezer and I call out to him, "Auger, help me." And suddenly he's right beside me. I swear he teleports sometimes.

I lift the towel off of Jill's wrist and immediately feel tears well up in my eyes. She's really cut herself deep this time, I can see white in the wound and I hope I'm not seeing bone. Oh Jill. You really do look dead.

"Auger, do something please," I say. I could never be a surgeon, I'd get all weepy every time I had to do an operation. "Help her."

Auger doesn't say anything for a moment. I can tell he's struggling, I don't need to take my eyes off Jill to know it. "Pete..." he starts. "Peter, I'm not a doctor." And I swear to god there's *sadness* in his voice. I stand up and grab him gently by the shoulders, noticing for the first time that he is literally *covered* in blood, like in *Carrie* except for his hands which somehow are immaculately clean. He won't make eye contact but I wasn't expecting him to anyway. "Please," I say. "You can do it, I know you can. Jill is our friend and she needs us... she needs you to help her right now." I'm saying this to someone I just watched chop another human being to ribbons, but that doesn't matter. He can put her back together the same as he tore that man apart.

He hasn't said anything yet, he's just staring at Jill as she lies on my bed and pulls in labored breaths. "Auger!" I shout, shaking him a bit. He looks up at my face but not into my eyes. "Bring her into my room," he says. "Help me lift her."

Auger moves over to Jill's lower half and positions himself, telling me to support her head while we carry her. I do my best as we raise her gently up off my bed and take her into Auger's room, which for the first time in memory is not only unlocked but open. The whole thing is covered in plastic, like the tent Peter Coyote kept E.T. in. There's an operating table in the center of the floor, and we carry Jill over to it and set her on top. Auger opens his closet and takes out two heavy blankets which he tosses to me, then wheels out an I.V. drip and snaps gloves onto his hands. He swabs Jill's arm at the elbow and inserts the tube as I cover her with the blankets.

"What're you giving her?" I ask.

"Saline," Auger says. "Nutrients. Find some gloves in the closet."

I do as I'm told. The gloves are in a box in plain sight, so I get a pair and pull them on. I turn back to Auger and see he's cleaning the cut on Jill's wrist, dropping a few bits of used swabs to the plastic below. The blood is encrusted, rust colored. She did this a while ago, maybe when it was still daylight. "What do you want me to do?" I ask.

"Stitches," he says. "Top drawer." I open the drawer and can't make any sense of what's inside. "Auger, I don't know what I'm looking at," I say. He appears beside me, teleporting again, and gets what he needs, handing me some swabs as he does so. "Finish cleaning her up," he says to me. So I do.

"Hey Pete," Jill says. I freeze for the third time this evening, holding her damaged arm in my hands. I look up at her and she's trying to smile, her eyes are barely open but she's looking right back at me. "Are you dead too?"

I'm not sure if I've been crying the whole time, but I definitely am now.

Six

It's about three thirty in the morning and some of Jill's color has started to come back, so basically she looks like somebody that *just* died as opposed to somebody that died *yesterday*. I've been sitting on a chair next to her in Auger's room for maybe an hour now. She passed right back out after being awake for just a moment and then Auger came over and tied her arm closed with some cat gut. Then he told me to stay and watch her, which is sort of like asking Eddie Murphy to continue being black.

The cops came to our apartment complex a little while ago, I saw their lights from Auger's window. They lingered for a bit, talking to whomever it was that called them, and then they quietly left. Not even so much as a knock on our door. In the movies if someone kills a person outside in plain view of an entire neighborhood, they get caught, right? At least most of the time, depending on what kind of movie it is. Is it really possible that not a single person saw Auger out there but me? And what about the veritable mountain of evidence he must have left in front of our building?

I ask myself that even though I know the answer. The cab driver's body is in here, stuffed in the chest freezer in our kitchen. That was what Auger was up to when I heard him shuffling around while I was in my room with Jill, it has to be. The only question left is what did Auger do with the taxi? He couldn't have left it sitting in the parking lot, so he must have taken it somewhere. He disappeared right after he was finished with Jill, so by now he could be in the next state with it. Or maybe he took it around the corner and pushed it into the lake, who knows? There's so much about Auger that I find I'd rather not think about right now, so I'm finished speculating. He's not here in the apartment, and that's fine with me.

Every shred of good sense in my body is screaming at me to get Jill to the hospital while every ounce of self preservation is keeping us locked in this room. The battle is quite epic, I'm sure it would make an awesome movie. If I call 911 right now all three of us are going to jail tonight, end of story. Auger and I would likely end up in *prison* shortly thereafter. And they'd take one look at the scars on

Jill's arms and throw her in some program until they decide she's ready to go back to her life, and while that might help her some I can't say it's what she *needs* and I damn sure know it's not what she *wants*. She could've called an ambulance for herself but instead she climbed into an evil taxi cab, butt naked and covered in blood and vomit, and drove across town to *us*, to *me*. She trusted me that much, so I'm not going to screw it up for her.

Auger's room is less than homey, I must admit. It looks like a giant condom, everything is covered in plastic. He doesn't even have any furniture besides the table that Jill is currently laying on and an empty silver tray that looks like it should be cluttered with surgical tools. Oh, and a cot that's folded up in the far corner. It's like minimalist Shakespeare in here. He spends all his time in this room, what the hell does he *do* all day? Maybe he has some board games in his closet.

"Pete," Jill says, snapping me back to attention. She's staring up at me, a little more warmth in her cheeks than when I first saw her tonight. She still looks like a china doll wrapped in tissue paper, swaddled on Auger's table under one of those cheap hospital sheets gone rigid with too much starch.

"Hey Jillybean," I say, faking a little more enthusiasm than I mean to. "How are you feeling?"

She contemplates this for a moment, weakly moving her head to look around Auger's room. "Like I'm in a giant condom," she says finally. "Now I know what all my unborn siblings felt like. Where are we? Please tell me you didn't take me to the hospital."

I laugh. She seems cogent, which is awesome. "No, ah, this is Auger's room," I tell her. "Do you remember anything? Do you know how you got here?"

Jill's eyes go soft and she pulls her lips tight in disdain, half jokingly and half not. "Yep," she says. "I walked for a while and fell down, somebody put me in a cab, the driver tried to rape me and I bit his right nut off. So, you know, a glass of water and some mouthwash would be pretty great if you can spare it."

Jill is amazing this way; she truly is not afraid of anything or anyone but herself. She could've just come here from Food Lion and it would probably be having the same effect on her. "Yea, I think so. I've got a bottle of Scope somewhere around here."

She smiles, looks down at her wrist and brushes the bandage with her fingertips. "Auger stitched me up *and* let me stay in his room? Wow, I feel like the *president*. Is he here?"

I shake my head. "He had to… he had to go somewhere. I don't know when he'll be back, you know how he is." The fact that my roommate is so mystical suddenly became useful for the first time I can remember.

Jill nods. "Yea, I know how he is. I have to make him something *really* cool for doing all this. What else does he like besides burritos?"

I start to say something I shouldn't and stop myself just in time. Instead, I shrug my shoulders and offer, "Maybe just make him a card?"

Jill gives me a weird look that I completely deserve but doesn't reply. She tugs at the IV tube in her arm, ruffles the sheet a little, runs her hand along the side of the operating table. "Where the *hell* does he get all this stuff?" she asks. "He has his own *hospital* in here. He could start a private practice."

It occurs to me that I have no idea where Auger could even *find* the equipment he has in his room, let alone how he managed to collect so much of it. Maybe he *does* have patients, some kind of under the table deal for people that either can't or won't go to the hospital. It makes a strange amount of sense now that I think about it; Auger *has* mentioned that he doesn't have the money for proper medical schooling, yet he's always studying and taking basic courses, sometimes even *re*taking courses that he's already completed. Not to mention he's converted his bedroom into a field hospital. None of that would be cheap, so he has to be getting the money from somewhere. A clandestine medical practice could be fairly close to the truth.

Or maybe he just kills people and robs them. This last thought gives me a shudder. But no, that can't be it. Tonight was different, the cab driver deserved it. Didn't he? After what we saw and what Jill just told me, it seems justified. Auger doesn't just go around killing people, he can't even look me in the eyes to tell me the toilet's backed up. No, that's ridiculous, there's another way, another perfectly reasonable source for Auger's money, probably something obvious that just hasn't dawned on me, maybe a rich aunt. It's none of my business anyway.

"Maybe he did," I say to Jill. "This is the first time I've ever been in here, too."

Jill nods slightly, tugs at her sheets again. "You saw me naked, huh."

I laugh again. "Yep. We'll have to do that again sometime when you're not covered in blood."

"I'll see what I can do," Jill says, coughing a little. "Can I have that water now?"

I go into the kitchen to oblige her request, but when I see the chest freezer I stop. There isn't anything unusual about it, no splatter-movie streak of blood running down the side, no protruding limbs, no chains or locks. It looks about as non-threatening as any other major appliance. I wish I could just lift the lid and find fish sticks and ice cream inside. But I know that's not the case, which is exactly why I walk straight over to it and open it up.

The cab driver is nestled inside, covered in ice and countless trash bags that Auger has lain over top of him. He'd be staring straight up at me if he still had eyes. Instead, two black holes settled into an old dead face are looking up and out into nothing. Auger cut his mandible off, I saw that much outside, so right now the driver's ruined body is frozen in exactly half of a scream, his thick purple tongue lying free on the ice like a cow's in a butcher shop. I gently close the freezer and get Jill her glass of water.

"So are we going to have to talk to the cops?" she asks after taking the glass from me and gulping it all down. "Did they show up? Has anyone called them?"

I scratch my head. "Ah, they came," I say. "I don't think we're going to have to talk to them, at least not if we're lucky."

Of course Jill doesn't understand, and she tells me as much with the look on her face. "Well what about the cab driver?" she asks. "I mean, *I* think we're even, but..."

"I, ah, wouldn't worry about him anymore," I say. I could lie, but what's the point? "He's sort of... dead."

Jill blinks incredulously. "He's dead?" Suddenly her face drops. "Oh god, did I kill him?! Did he bleed to death? Holy shit, I didn't mean to kill him! He totally *deserved* what happened, but I didn't mean to kill him!"

She starts hyperventilating, repeating "Oh no, oh no, oh no" over and over again. I try to get a word in but she doesn't seem to hear me, so I wrap my arms around her and hug her tight, try speaking into her ear which seems to work. Her breathing slows down but I can feel her heart and it's still going about a hundred miles an hour.

"I didn't mean to kill anyone," Jill says weakly. "I didn't mean to, I don't want to go to jail."

I squeeze her tighter, rubbing her shoulders gently. I kiss her cheek and tell her, "It's okay, you didn't kill him. Auger did."

Seven

Auger has box after box of notebooks in his closet, each one completely full of notes, sketches, money order slips, even hand drawn maps of the neighboring cities with plotted routes in red marker. I'm pulling these boxes out one after another, opening them and taking inventory while Jill flips through the notebooks and reads sections aloud. We're like two kids that just found where their Christmas presents are hidden.

"'Subject has a shattered right kneecap and a two inch gash in the left pectoral,'" Jill recites. She's wearing some of my old clothes, a brown hooded sweatshirt left over from when I dressed up as a Jedi to see *Revenge of the Sith* and a pair of my jeans holding onto her waist for dear life by a belt on about the fifth or sixth notch. She is no less adorable, I might add. "'I crushed the knee with a baseball bat swung approximately two feet with moderate force,'" she continues.

"'Fragmentation is likely but impossible to determine pre-surgery without an x-ray.'"

"I'm surprised he doesn't have an x-ray in here," I say, tearing open another box and finding more stacks of notebooks inside. Behind me Jill reads through more of the passage silently, scanning the lines of Auger's immaculate handwriting with her finger. "Well apparently Auger fixed this guy," Jill says. "Drugged him and left him at a convenience store when he was done. Tsk."

"Nice private practice," I say. "You know, *some* people might actually be a little bothered by this." Quite the opposite, Jill couldn't wait to get off of the operating table when I told her what Auger had done tonight. I didn't tell her about the body in the chest freezer, but once I got her some clothes from my room she started tearing through Auger's closet and has been playing Nancy Drew ever since.

"Well it *is* a little weird," Jill says. She picks up a new notebook and starts flipping through it. "Man, he's got *insanely* detailed sketches of everything he's ever tried. It's kind of impressive."

Like I mentioned earlier, Jill is not afraid of anything or anyone but herself. "Don't you feel at least a *little* uneasy?" I ask. "He's been doing all this right in front of us for *years*. While we were in the next room. While I was *asleep*. That doesn't freak you out?"

Jill shrugs. "Why should it? I mean, he *could* be making all of this up, we don't know. And besides, this is *Auger*. It's not like he's going to operate on *you*."

I stop. *Operate on you.*

"What're the dates in those books you're looking at?" I ask. "The ones in the box I just gave you?"

"Uh, June of this year," Jill says. "Why?"

"Help me find this month."

October

(Several illustrations of a heavily scarred wrist)

...The subject's goal is not to seriously injure himself, but to incur such an injury that would have the outward appearance of being life-threatening. His motivations are irrelevant to the procedure and will not be discussed here...

(Diagram of a male torso, with labels and measurements on both sides of the belly)

...I obtained several different knives from the subject's workplace to determine which would be the ideal instrument for him to use. I need to carefully plot each point of the procedure and present it to the subject in great detail, as the slightest error on either of our parts could be dire...

(Illustrations of numerous chef's knives of varying lengths)

...Today's trial was sloppy and poorly executed. Much more precision will be needed to properly meet the desired end. Subject's internal organs were spared but narrowly, which leads me to believe that he will almost certainly rupture them when he attempts the procedure himself. To prevent this I have removed the subject's kidney, which should provide him a modest safety net. He is unlikely to notice during his recovery...

(Detailed diagram of the human kidney)

(Several illustrations of a heavily scarred wrist)

...That's what friends are for...

(Several illustrations of a heavily scarred wrist)

Auger

One

I took the taxi around the corner to the lake that is just behind our apartment building, put the car in neutral and pushed it down the bank into the water after breaking out both windshields and all the side windows so that it would sink faster. I washed my face with a few cupped handfuls from the lake, then walked quickly back to our door and inspected the surrounding area beneath the hum of the entryway's dim exterior light. Finding that I had not missed anything, I went quietly back inside. I assumed Jill was sleeping, and perhaps Pete as well, so I did not want to disturb them. Moving as silently as I could manage, I separated the driver's remains inside the chest freezer and collected them into garbage bags. The ensuing mess will keep inside the freezer, but should it leak out onto the floor for some reason we have a mop in the hall closet. The bags were then carried down to Pete's car and placed in the trunk.

I'm having more trouble than usual tonight. I didn't trust myself to help Jill. There's no reason I shouldn't have, I have hundreds of hours of study and training to my credit and hers was a fairly simple procedure. But I felt something, perhaps because of the attack she suffered, that made me hesitate, a doubt that delayed my reaction. I shame my field with that behavior, but I cannot deny it was a pure and natural impulse. I was concerned about my ability to help Jill and apprehensive about what might happen should I fail. I will read through my notes, but I am certain this has never happened to me. The doubt that suddenly plagued me, the uncertainty looking over my shoulder like an austere headmaster pressured me during the procedure. Jill's words from dinner, *that's what friends are for*, kept repeating in my brain. Normally I work for my own benefit and progression, and I still believe that is the only honest focus for anyone's efforts in life, but tonight I found myself wanting to succeed for Jill's sake. I didn't want to fail *her*. This is very difficult for me. I need to consider this situation further at the appropriate time. I also need a new saw.

I close the trunk and walk back inside for a final time before I depart with the taxi driver's body. Content I've left nothing of consequence behind, I go to the door, but stop when I hear Pete and Jill talking in my room. I should check on them. Pete doesn't have the knowledge to act if something should go wrong during Jill's recovery, though I don't anticipate that anything will. Just a quick glance before I leave to make sure she's progressing smoothly.

Pete and Auger

Auger has a box in here that is full of jewelry. Watches, bracelets, earrings, even *wedding rings*. Jill peeks in beside me and gasps. Nice private practice. He should name it Auschwitz.

The door to my room is open so I can see from here that Jill has gotten off the operating table and disconnected the IV drip, which she really shouldn't have done yet.

I hear the plastic floor rustle and look up to see Auger standing in the doorway of the room. He stares at us, unblinking, his face as expressionless as always. Jill tries to say something to him but I just stare back. I think this is about to get very bad.

They're reading my notes, which is slightly irritating because I had them carefully organized and was planning on reading through them later. Now several books are scattered across the floor. It's my fault really, if I didn't want my things disturbed I should've kept them locked up, so I can't blame Pete and Jill for their curiosity. Although I'm worried that Pete might have found my writings on his procedure. I have yet to tell him that I removed his kidney. He might be angry about that.

"So who are you going to cut up next?" I ask Auger. "Me or Jill?" I throw the box of jewelry down at his feet, sending several glittering accessories spilling onto the plastic. "Should I empty out my pockets into that box first and save you some trouble?"

Yes, Pete has definitely read about his procedure. I look to Jill for assistance but she doesn't offer any to me. "Hey Pete," she says instead, "calm down, okay? Let's calm down for a second. We're all friends here, right?"

"He's not my fucking friend!" I shout, not taking my eyes off Auger. I'm hiding my fear with anger; I'm actually so terrified right now that I can't move. I *do* need to calm down but I can't. Auger hasn't spoken, I don't think he's even *blinked*. Jill says, "Come on, let's all go out to the couch and sit down, okay? *We are friends*. Things are just a little weird right now but it's going to be fine." She moves towards Auger. I'm not feeling good about that.

I'm having trouble. I feel ashamed but I don't know why. Pete won't look away, I don't like it when people look at me. I put my hand in my pocket to grab the pin but it isn't there, it's never there.

Jill puts her hands on Auger's face and turns it towards her, looking directly into his eyes. "Auger," she says to him, "I had a terrible fucking night and you helped me, so I know that means something. I can speak for myself and tell you that I've read through all your stuff and I don't care about what you've done, only about what you've done for me. Okay?" She starts to unzip his jacket, covered in blood that has long dried and turned brown. "Here, take this off, you're looking like I did when I got here," she says.

"That's what friends are for," I say to Jill, because she's right. I care about her, it matters to me what happens to her, that's why I keep helping her when I normally wouldn't. That's why I felt the doubt tonight, because I didn't want to fail. I don't try to stop her when she slides my jacket off, even though I know what is about to happen. This is the happiest moment of my life.

He is *covered* in steel, a bandolier of surgical tools wrapped around his torso like a metal skeleton. The notebooks, the wedding rings and the dead body in the chest freezer flash through my mind in an instant, and now Auger stands before us looking like a cross between Jack the Ripper and Rambo. Jill is still standing next to him, dropping his jacket to the floor. She hasn't looked up yet, hasn't seen what she's done. A new image splashes into my mind, one of Auger and Jill in this very room, her tied to the operating table and him cutting her open just so he can put her back together and dump her body at a convenience store somewhere. That's why he draws maps with plotted routes, that's why he bought the damn freezer, that's why he does *everything*. I didn't know before or maybe I just ignored it, but not this time Auger. You took my damn kidney but you can't have her, you're not going to cut her up. I guess I say this aloud because they both turn in time to see me lunge forward.

Pete shoves Auger through the doorway and out into the common room as Jill cries out in shock and protest. The two trip on each other's feet, suddenly entangled, and crash to the floor next to the television. Pete grabs Auger by the collar and punches him in the cheek, careful to avoid the steel strapped around Auger's torso. Pete stands up quickly, kicking his roommate hard in the back as he does so, and moves to Jill, shoving his car keys into her hands.

"*What are you doing?*" she shouts.

"Take my car and get out of here!" Pete says.

"Pete, stop it! What the hell is wrong with you?!"

"What's wrong with *me*?" Pete is about to continue this thought when Auger, having risen from the common room floor, lifts forty pounds of television set into the air and smashes it into Pete's back. The screen implodes with an electrical hiss and Pete flies forward, knocking into Jill and sending them both spinning off their feet, trapping her beneath the weight of his body. She struggles to free herself then stops, feeling Auger's presence looming overhead. She looks up into his eyes and he doesn't look away this time, but in those two silver pools Jill sees nothing at all.

"Auger," she says. "Auger, I think Pete is out. Help me, please? Can you help me get up?" She wriggles an arm free and reaches up to him. Auger stares at her hand but does not move. "Please?" she says again, straining her hand towards him.

Auger finally grabs her by the wrist and pulls her from underneath Pete's unmoving body. She winces a bit; glass from the television screen, embedded in Auger's palm, is now grinding into her skin. *Good thing this isn't the bad wrist*, she thinks, glancing briefly at the bandage on her opposite arm.

"Thanks," Jill says to Auger, on her feet again. Auger doesn't respond, instead he continues to stare at Pete's prostrate form. "Hey, no more fighting please," she says to him while gently touching his shoulder. "You guys lost your tempers and that's fine, it's ok, but I think he might really be hurt." Her voice is shaking a bit and her eyes are wet, but she is doing her best to appear calm and in control. "So... so why don't you guys just stop and we can talk, okay?"

Still no words from Auger. He steps over Pete and collects his jacket off the plastic covered floor in his room, slides his arms through the sleeves and zips it up. Then he crosses back into the common room, stepping over Pete once more. As Auger does this, Pete's arm strikes up and snatches Auger by the ankle, yanking hard and throwing him against the bathroom doorframe. The wooden frame cracks loudly like a shotgun blast and Auger slides down to one knee. Pete struggles to his feet and stumbles for a moment, then grabs Auger by the shoulders and pushes him into the bathroom, towards the sliding-glass shower door.

"*Oh no,*" Jill says softly.

With a guttural yell, Pete sends Auger flying through the glass and into the bathtub. Shards rain down in a torrent, pounding against Auger's body like a waterfall. Metal bits of frame boomerang out onto the tiled floor beneath the sink. Jill starts to run forward but Pete stops her, holding her strongly as she tries to wrench free from his grasp.

"*Let go of me, Pete!*" she snaps.

"Jill, he *kills* people!" Pete shouts, holding tight against her struggles. "He kills them for *no reason!*"

"That doesn't give you the right to hurt him!" Jill cries with a sob, relaxing slightly but still resolute. "And what he did tonight wasn't for no reason!"

Finally she breaks, the weight of everything she's been through that evening comes spilling out of her eyes and into Pete's chest where she buries her face. Pete's hold turns nurturing and he hugs her to him, and for a moment they are just two people comforting each other.

A hand grips the lip of the bathtub, running a thin line of red down to pool in the cracks of the tiles below. The black mass within the tub stirs, sending bits of glass tinkling against the porcelain.

"Jill," Pete says softly, staring into the bathroom. "Take my keys and get out now."

"No," she replies, still pressing her face into Pete's chest.

Auger rises from the bathtub with shards running off him like water, a twisted Lady of the Lake from legend. Blood pours from dozens of cuts on his face, neck and hands; his eyes are completely masked by it. He reaches into his jacket and unsheathes a battered surgical saw, missing two teeth but looking no less sharp than the day it was made.

"Actually, we should both probably leave," Pete says.

Jill

One

This is the first time I've ever driven Pete's car for a reason *other* than him being too drunk to do it himself, which is invigorating in a *Driving Miss Daisy* sort of way. He doesn't seem to be hurt so bad, there's a knot on his head and a giant bruise where the TV hit right between his shoulder blades that looks like a mutant California raisin, but he's kind of moving around a little so I guess that means his spine is okay. I really have no idea, I probably paralyzed him for life by tossing him into this car. Still, I don't regret not going to college.

The drive to my house is a lot faster than the *walk*, let me tell you. Most of tonight is a blur to me, and to be honest I'm still having some of that underwater feeling so maybe I shouldn't be driving. I remember all the important things, though, like the cop and the cab driver and all that. I was freaked out about it at first when I thought I'd killed him, but when Pete told me what Auger had done, I really didn't mind that much. Does that make me wrong? Like evil? I mean, I could never kill anyone myself, but I definitely think there are some people that deserve to die, ones that just *hurt* other people for no reason, and that guy probably deserved it because I doubt tonight was the first time he ever tried to rape somebody. So there's one less creepy asshole in the world, so what? Should I feel bad about it? I mean, I was in no shape to *stop* Auger, but the fact that I haven't called the police and probably won't anytime soon makes me an accomplice, doesn't it? I think it does. Ugh, I should've watched more *Law and Order* when George had it on all the time.

I'm being kind of a hypocrite, I know. By my definition of people that deserve to die, Auger and his "medicine macabre" should probably on the list right next to the grabby cabbie. But he's *different*, I don't know. If I believe everything I read in his journals as fact, then he's just a straight-up murderer, no question. But maybe some of it isn't true, maybe he's made some parts up. Or maybe all of it, I don't know. It's possible. All that jewelry he could've just stolen or found somewhere. And I've been trying so hard to get him to *like* me that I really don't want him to be bad. I mean, he's *Auger*. He likes burritos.

I don't really have much of a plan. I figured I would take Pete to my house for the time being, my parents aren't going to be back for at least another week. They sometimes decide to stay away longer if they're particularly enjoying themselves, so I'll pray for good weather in wherever the hell they are this time. Spain, I think. Anyway, Pete can stay with me, because I think leaving him in that apartment is a mistake. He and Auger would probably fight again, or the police might show up and that would be like an episode of *Benny Hill* without the British whimsy. Gross.

We're pulling up next to my house right now. I feel like it's been about seventeen hours since I was here last, but it's still dark out so I know that's probably an exaggeration. Pete is lying in the backseat with one of the lap belts holding him still so he doesn't roll forward and bounce off of the driver's seat. I don't want him to be *more* paralyzed, after all. I get out of the car and walk around to the side to open it up and drag him out when I hear someone's voice.

"Excuse me miss?" a man says. I jump a little and turn to see who just scared a little bit of pee into the pair of Pete's jeans I'm wearing. Good god, it's a frigging cop.

"Ms. Edison?" he continues. He starts walking towards me from his car, which was parked like *right* behind me and I didn't even see it. "It's Officer Owens, from earlier tonight. Do you remember me?"

Ugh. Shoo, cop, shoo. "Yea, I remember," I say, stepping away from Pete's car ever so slightly.

"Is everything okay?" Owens asks. He's being completely non-threatening but as you might imagine I'm beginning to feel the steady grip of panic. I try to play it off and kind of shrug my shoulders and look around a bit. "Yea why, does something look wrong?" I say as nonchalant as I can.

Owens stares at me for a minute. "No," he says. "Your... ah, *condition* earlier make me think that you might be in some kind of trouble, so I thought I'd drive by your house to make sure you got home safe." He spots Pete in the back. "Your friend have too much fun tonight?"

I spot a way out of this. "Yea, he sure did," I say with a laugh about as authentic and natural as the canned ones they play on sitcoms. "That's where I was going earlier, I had to go get his car and pick him up." I exhale sharply. "Some night!"

Owens raises an eyebrow and I curse inwardly. "I see you changed your clothes too," he says.

"Yea, well my coat was *dirty*, you know?" I say. "Gotta look good for... for my *man* there."

He looks at Pete then turns back to me. "Alright then, Ms. Edison," he says. "Have a good night." And he walks away, back to his cruiser.

Wow, that was a lot easier than I thought it would be. Maybe it's good that I didn't watch *Law and Order*, I'd probably have a ton of shattered misconceptions right about now. I pop the door open and put my arms under Pete's shoulders. "Come on," I say, pulling him with a fantastic effort out onto the sidewalk. He's not that heavy, but I'm built like a pixie stick, so I think I deserve applause. He's sort of snapping out of it, which is good because I'd have quite a time getting him inside if he was *all* dead weight. I get my head under his armpit and start walking him to the front door.

"Wha… his is down… bubbles…" Pete mumbles. I file that away for future teasing reference as we struggle the rest of the way up my steps.

Two

Good lord my house is a mess. Particularly my bathroom, it looks like a damn *crime scene*. I knocked a bunch of stuff over downstairs and there's blood on *everything*, it's going to take me like three days to clean it all up. I really screwed up this time, I'm such an idiot. If you think about it, *nothing* that's happened tonight would've happened if I could just stop *hating* myself for ten damn minutes. If I hadn't cut my arm up like Edward Scissorhands, everything would be *fine*, we'd all be friends and things would be like they always are.

Which is awful. I mean, Pete and I are completely miserable. Auger probably is, too. We're like the people stuck in steerage on the *Titanic*, drowning slowly in our rooms. I said before, I don't mind waiting tables and living in an apartment for the rest of my life, but I want to be *happy* with myself, you know? I want to love where I am and what I'm doing, and right now I just don't.

I'm going to ask Pete, just grow a pair and *ask* him like an adult. He's asleep in my bed right now, but as soon as he's up, we're going to talk and I'm going to ask him to move away with me somewhere. I think we'd be good for each other, you know? Maybe he'd inspire me to start writing again, and we could do something together. I think that would be great for both of us. I walk upstairs to my room after cleaning up a bit and just sit on the edge of my bed and watch him for a while. He really is a good guy. Jeez, that bruise on his back is nasty, he's sleeping shirtless on his side with that ugly purple thing between his shoulders facing me. I touch my nose instinctively, which has turned the same shade of black and blue after I fell on my face earlier. It hurts, sure, but I guess it makes me feel closer to Pete somehow. I don't know.

Pete rolls over and sees me staring at him. "Hey Jill," he says. "What's up?"

I smile. "Oh you know, the usual. One of us is crippled in bed again."

He sits up. "I'm not crippled," he says. "I just got knocked out, I think. What happened?"

"Um, Auger hit you with the TV and then slammed your head in the bathroom door."

We kind of blink at each other for a moment.

"Yea I guess he did," he says. "Jesus, that hurts." He gingerly feels the bump on his head and starts trying to rub his back, but the bruise is totally beyond his reach so he looks pretty funny right now.

"Here, lay back," I tell him, leaning over and pushing on his chest until he does as I say. "I can get you some ice? I think we have a heating pad somewhere, too."

"Yea, okay," Pete says. I'm kind of sitting on top of him, looking down into his eyes, and neither one of us is saying anything so it's turning into one of *those* moments. I don't want to move and I don't think he wants me to either, so I figure *what the hell* and I lean down and kiss him, and he kisses me back and suddenly I feel the happiest I've been since I can't remember when.

Auger

One

I step forward out of the bathtub towards Pete and Jill, glass crunching lightly beneath my shoes like dead leaves. He bodily lifts Jill and puts her aside, I suppose to move her out of harm's way in some vain display of chivalry. It makes no difference to me.

Pete tries to kick me, throwing his leg clumsily out in an attempt to keep his body out of reach of the saw I'm currently holding in my left hand. I easily swat his foot aside, striking him in the shin with my right hand and sending him off balance. He quickly tries to reset himself and throws a hasty backhand in the general direction of my face. I feint back, again avoiding his attack with minimal effort, and immediately strike him in his exposed shoulder with the dull edge of the saw. His arm goes limp instantly and I seize it with both hands, dropping my saw as I do so. I pull him towards me and throw my knee upwards, making direct contact with the stab wound in his belly and forcing the air out of his lungs. Pete doubles over. Still holding his arm with my right hand, I take my left hand and grab the back of his neck, then hook my left leg around his feet and throw him facedown into the bathroom.

Jill rushes at me and grabs me around the torso with surprising strength, saying something to me that I simply do not hear. I push her away and she falls against the broken television in the common room, crying out as some of the glass is crushed beneath her outstretched palms. I didn't mean for that to happen.

I turn back to Pete, lying on his stomach with his head just inside the bathroom, his shallow breathing fogging a small layer of condensation on the tiles beneath his face. I slam the door against his skull violently, nearly tearing the doorknob out as I do so and sending a shockwave that shudders through his entire body. I pick my saw up and kneel next to Pete's unconscious form, resting the teeth on the back of his neck.

And I stop. I stand instead, replacing the saw in my wrap, and walk over to Jill in the common room. She is pulling small shards out of her hands with great anguish and did not see what nearly transpired. I reach a hand out to her and say, "Jill."

She looks up at me, startled, and then tentatively accepts. I lift her to her feet, but she doesn't let go right away.

"Please stop," she says. "I don't care about anything you've done, Auger, just please stop now."

I stare at her for a long time. My head is beginning to hurt, I can feel myself starting to panic for reasons that I don't understand. I pull away from her and hurry towards the front door.

"Auger, help me please?" Jill says shakily. "If… if you've really hurt Pete, I don't know what to do."

I pause but I don't turn around to face her. "Neither do I," I say. "I'm not a doctor." Then I walk out the door into the night, leaving them both behind me.

Pete

One

I'm having a dream about Jill and I. We're on a road trip someplace south and it's summertime, all the windows are open and I'm looking over at her in the seat beside me. She's wearing big sunglasses and her hair is a little longer, blowing crazily in the wind as we roar down the interstate. Both of us are laughing about something, I'm given no clear indication what. To be honest, I don't care; I'm enjoying this too much. She really looks amazing, just laughing and laughing as the sunlight pours in all around us and paints her soft skin gold. I reach out and touch her face, and she bends her head to trap my hand between her cheek and her shoulder.

Then I wake up in the dark, only Jill is still here, naked and wrapped around me underneath the blanket, clutching me like driftwood and sleeping peacefully. I turn into her and kiss her hard on the mouth and she wakes up and smiles at me.

You're a smart kid. You can guess what happens next.

Two

I've been staying at Jill's for a day now. My head still hurts like someone hit me in the face with a microwave, and my back still hurts like... well, like someone hit me with a TV. Really I just feel like I've been assaulted by major appliances.

We spent the first morning cleaning up the disaster relief zone she'd made of her house after cutting herself open the night before. When I saw the bathroom I almost started crying, so Jill sent me downstairs to straighten up the kitchen, which was far less graphic. We haven't talked about it really, not yet anyway, not aloud. But it feels like we both have this understanding about it, like we've been communicating telepathically on the subject. Honestly, I don't *need* for us to ever have a conversation about it unless she wants to. I can do my best to see that she doesn't ever feel that low again, but I won't expect her to explain herself to me. I contemplated this as I was mopping her blood off the kitchen floor, so it was all very existential. The irony was not lost on me, I assure you.

It really didn't take us all that long to finish, we were done in time for lunch. Neither one of us had eaten in probably 24 hours, so we ordered the biggest pizza ever constructed by mortal hands and ate the whole damn thing on her couch, where upon her insistence I finally watched *The Land Before Time* while shoveling fourteen pounds of dough and cheese down my gullet. And I must admit, it's a pretty sweet movie, although some parts of it are deeply depressing. For instance, I wept when the tyrannosaurus died. It just wasn't fair.

Three

I need to go to the hospital and see if Auger really *did* take my kidney out. There are stitches on both the front and back of my lower torso, but I'm not sure if the knife went all the way through when he stabbed me so I can't consider that indisputable evidence. And to be honest, I'm clueless when it comes to medical science; I don't know if the doctor would x-ray me to check if the kidney was still there or try to call it on the phone and see if it answered. At my level of comparative ignorance, neither procedure would surprise me.

And honestly, what would it matter if Auger *did* take it? It'd be something I would need to know for future reference, of course, but other than that I don't imagine it affecting my daily life in any meaningful way. Organs can be funny like that, as is my understanding. Maybe in another two hundred years the left kidney will become vestigial and I'll be hailed as a pioneer, like George Washington Carver or Thomas Dolby. I think what I'll probably do is just give the doctor a heads-up the next time I go in for a checkup. "Hey doc, just thought you should know before we get started that I *may* or *may not* have both of my kidneys, so tuck that under your cap and we are ready to *roll*."

Four

We're taking a few days off of Auger and the apartment, although I know I'm going to eventually have to go back if for nothing else than my clothes and my deodorant (I've been using Jill's and, while effeminate, it smells *terrific*). I'm still on my Todd-enforced suspension from The Loaf, but that only lasts for another three days. Sometime in between now and then I'm going to have to go and get my things, and possibly face Auger if he's there. I'm not looking forward to it, to say the least.

Everything at Jill's has been *great*, though. It's been like a vacation for both of us, although we haven't even left the house. We talk all day, watch movies, play Nintendo. We've spent every waking moment together and it's really cleared my head from the fog I've been wandering through these past three years or so. Needless to say, I think we should've gotten together a *long* time ago, but I'm glad that it's happening now. I feel like a huge weight has been lifted. I still haven't mustered up the courage to ask her about moving, although I'm pretty confident I'll get to it, with the way everything's been going.

You know what? Auger can go straight to hell. I don't care about him or whatever he's doing, because for the first time in a while I'm just fine and he's not going to ruin it for me.

Jill

One

    Pete is sitting at our kitchen table drinking a glass of orange juice and scribbling something down in a composition notebook he must've found somewhere in our house. I just got out of the shower so my hair is still wet and I'm a little cold, but I don't feel like running back upstairs just yet to get a sweatshirt. I'm *way* too interested to see what he's up to, since he's been complaining about not being able to write lately just like me. Well, I haven't written anything in like four *years*, so maybe "lately" isn't the word for me, but whatever.

    "What're you up to?" I ask him. "And who said you could steal notebooks from my house, you sly boots?"

    He looks up, seriously concerned that I might actually *care* if he took a notebook without asking. "Oh, sorry," he says. "I didn't think you would mind... I can buy you another one."

    I laugh. "Take it easy, Lee Harvey, I *don't* mind. How about instead of buying me a new notebook, you just tell me what you're putting in *that* one?" I sit down across from him and stare expectantly, just to be an asshole.

    "Um, okay," Pete says, and he kind of starts rustling the pages in front of him, I guess in an effort to stall. "I... ah, I don't really know what it is yet. I've had a bunch of different ideas bouncing around in my head for a couple of years that I never did anything with, so I'm just kind of writing everything out and seeing what I can do with it."

    "Ooh," I say. "Can I see them? Do you mind? You *do* owe me for the notebook, you know."

    "Um, sure, I guess," he says, sliding the book across the table.

    I can't think of anything else to say so I just smile really big at Pete, one of those huge goofy smiles you usually save for someone like Santa Claus, and start reading the shaky handwriting he's laid down in a composition notebook that I didn't even know I *had*.

Two

It's a little later the same morning and the two of us are in my parents' backyard just screwing around, occasionally tossing a little football we found in the street back and forth but not really committed to a game of catch. I read all the ideas he wrote down earlier and they seemed pretty good with the exception of one that I didn't really understand. He's more talented than I knew, which is nice. I like pleasant surprises.

"It's been a long time since I tried, so I'm not sure how well I could string something together into an actual story," Pete is saying as he half-heartedly tosses me the tiny football. I catch it pretty easily, but I don't throw it back right away because I'm thinking about what he's just said. Finally I decide to just put myself out there, and I lob the ball back at him.

"I could help you," I say after he catches it. "If you want. Like co-write?"

Pete doesn't say anything right away so I keep going. "I mean, I haven't done anything in a while either, and I really want to get back into it. I remember you said it's something you'd like to try. I think it could be kind of cool, you know?"

I'm holding my breath but I hope he can't tell. He's clearly thinking about it, biting his lip a little while spinning the football in his hands. Good god, I have to believe this is somewhat related to what guys go through when they're down on one knee. Bless you, gentlemen, you deserve more credit.

"Yea," Pete says finally. "That'd be awesome, actually."

I'm so freaking excited that I don't even attempt to catch the ball when it comes back my way and it bounces right off my forehead. Precluding any subtlety, I sprint forward and jump into him, planting a big wet kiss on his lips. He tries to hold me but I feel his legs shudder and we both fall down on the grass. I'm laughing like an idiot the whole time.

"I don't think this is how they play in the NFL," Pete says, "unless the rules have changed or the players are really *great* friends."

Three

I've decided that the two of us need to get out of the house at least once before we have to go back to work, which isn't for two more days but we've already spent two almost exclusively indoors. I feel like we should have big eyes and no pigment like cave dwelling lizards or something. After a kitchen table discussion of what we should do (during which Pete said "Um…" about forty seven times), we decided to go out for lunch since we're both getting pretty tired of eating cereal and macaroni.

Pete is borrowing some of my dad's clothes, specifically an old white button-up that at best looks like something Dr. Who would wear. It's kind of amazing and gross at the same time. I don't even know why my dad *has* that shirt, maybe it was part of a costume, but it's the only one that sort of fits Pete so them's the breaks. At least he still has his own coat to put on over top of it.

I've been feeling pretty good since Auger sewed me up the other night. I was really weak the first day, but I think all my gears are turning properly now. I wonder what he's doing; actually, I've *been* wondering what he's doing ever since I brought Pete back to my house. I hope he's okay, I really do. I hope I see him again. It's funny, both Pete and I have scars to remember him by. Though to be fair, I've got scars *all over*. It's going to be an awesome story to tell if I ever have kids. "Wow Mommy, did you get attacked by a *bear*?" I think that's what I'm going to start telling people, actually. And if I ever get caught in a lie, I can say that I meant the bear as a metaphor for my own self-loathing.

That sounds like something Pete would say. I think he's rubbing off on me.

Lunch

Pete steps out of the front door followed by Jill, who stops to pull it closed and lock it behind her. She drops her keys into her coat pocket and tightens her scarf, teeth chattering slightly in the cold. Pete wraps an arm around her, rubbing some warmth into her shoulders, and the two walk down the steps to his car. He reaches out to open the passenger door for Jill but stops, his brow furrowing.

"Do you smell that?" he asks.

Jill sniffs and then groans with disgust. "Ugh, it smells like sewage or something. Do you have poop on your shoe?"

They both inspect the soles of their feet with surprising agility, but find no source for the offending odor.

"Wow," Pete says. "It smells like M. Night Shyamalan's *The Village* out here. I feel like we should call the fire department."

He opens the passenger door to let Jill into the car. As he does so, the stench becomes intensely foul as if he had just pried open a coffin lid. Pete gags and Jill covers her nose and mouth.

"Jeez, did a *raccoon* crawl into your car and die?" she says through her hand.

Pete looks at her for a moment. Suddenly his eyes go wide.

"Oh no," he says.

"What?" Jill asks, drawing her hand slowly away from her face. "What is it?"

Pete moves quickly to the back of the car, fumbling to unlock the trunk. "No, no, no, no, no!"

"Pete, *what* are you doing?" Jill says. "What's going on?"

He finally gets the key into the lock and turns it, lifting the lid to stare inside. The odor hits him like a freight train and he staggers back, coughing. Careful not to breathe through her nose, Jill steps cautiously up to the trunk to see several amorphous lumps wrapped in black trash bags laid neatly within. She walks backwards away from the car and towards Pete, absently rubbing the stitches on her arm through her jacket.

"Is that…" she says, not taking her eyes off the trunk.

"That's a dead cab driver," Pete says, bent over with his hands on his knees trying to catch his breath.

"Oh," Jill says, with the same inflection she might use if someone gave her a homemade birthday card. "I think maybe Auger has a key to your car?"

Pete straightens up. "Yea," he says. "I think so, too. Let's go ask him."

Jill turns to face him. "Back to the apartment?" she asks, then points at the trunk. "What about him?"

"I don't think he's going anywhere," Pete says. "We can drive…"

Jill stares at him.

"Ah, we could take a *taxi*…"

Jill continues to stare.

"The bus?" Pete offers finally.

Jill nods. "Yea, that one," she says. "At least on the bus, all the smelly people are still *alive*."

Pete moves past her, covering his nose with the back of his forearm, and slams the lid shut.

Bus

Pete and Jill sit on the bus together, he with his arm around her shoulder and she with her hands folded between her thighs and her knees turned in towards his body. Around them, various passengers are going about their own business, reading newspapers and talking on cell phones. Jill looks around at some of them, chewing her lip thoughtfully.

"I wonder if Auger ever operated on any of these people," she says, then notices a particularly scraggily looking man sitting in the back and adds, "Ooh, *he*

94

could use some work, for sure."

Pete surveys the crowd as well, considering her question. "I don't know," he says. "I guess he could have. What a weird experience that would be. Like, you have appendicitis and you're out on the town one day when all of a sudden BOOM. You wake up in a dumpster and you're all better except for a two inch gash on your head where Auger knocked you out with a hammer."

"Maybe he's a superhero," Jill says. "Like the Punisher. Maybe all his patients are sickos and drug dealers."

"No, that's probably not right at all," Pete says immediately. "Although the thought of Auger wearing a cape is pretty amazing."

"I know, right? If we see him, I'm going to tell him."

Pete blinks. "Tell him that he should have a cape?"

"No, that he should be a superhero," Jill says matter-of-factly. "He's already using your car as the batmobile. All he *needs* at this point is a cape."

They sit in silence for a few moments, bouncing up and down along with the bus as it lumbers to its next stop.

"So, ah, what *are* we going to say to him?" Jill asks. "'Come take care of this dead person'? I mean, it's not like he left *Chinese food* in your car."

Pete shrugs. "Yea, I guess so. I hadn't really thought of it, I was hoping it would come to me when I saw him."

Jill exhales sharply. "If what happened the other night is any indication, you don't think so well on your feet. Maybe I should talk to him instead."

Pete rests his chin on the top of her head, watching as the bus deposits some passengers and collects a few new ones before shuddering away from the curb.

"Yea," he says. "That's probably a good idea, I think he might still be mad at me. What're you going to say to him?"

Jill shakes her head. "I don't know, I'm hoping it comes to me when I see him."

Pete laughs and kisses her head as the bus drives on.

Maps

Pete breathes a sigh of equal parts relief and disappointment upon finding the apartment empty. Still, as he stands in the entryway he finds himself knocking on the open door again and calling Auger's name, just to be certain. Jill steps around him and walks inside, unraveling her scarf and putting her gloves into her jacket pocket.

"Hello?" she says. "Auger, are you here?"

"I already tried that," Pete says, closing the door. "I knocked, too."

"Yea well he's mad at you, remember?" Jill says, walking into the kitchen and sniffing the air tentatively. "It smells a *little* ripe in here," she says. "Not a zombie dog fart like your car, but still not quite Irish Spring. We should check it for body parts."

"If the lead detective will take a suggestion," Pete says, "I recommend looking in the chest freezer."

"Ooh, really?" Jill crosses quickly over to the freezer against the far wall of the kitchen and lifts the lid, peering inside for several moments.

"...*well?*" Pete says finally.

"Ah, maybe?" Jill says with a shrug. "I don't know if any of this counts as *parts*, but it's definitely *chunks*."

Frowning, Pete walks up next to her to see for himself. Pulpy bits of red are strewn across the interior walls of the freezer and along the ice inside.

"It almost looks like it could be jelly or something," Jill says with a breath. "So what do we do?"

Pete blinks. "Well, I guess we can unplug it and let the ice melt," he says. "We could run a hose from here to the sink so all the water goes straight down the drain."

"What about the... *pieces*, I guess?" Jill asks, gently rubbing her swollen nose.

"We just scrub the freezer out afterwards, I suppose," Pete says. "Or we could carry the whole thing down to the dumpster, either way." Pete closes the freezer and walks into the common room, stepping around the broken television and the shattered remains of its screen.

"Pete?" Jill calls after him. "If you start throwing his stuff away, he's just going to be mad at you *more*."

Pete stands examining the bathroom's broken doorframe and the collected debris of glass and metal and blood on the tiled floor within. "I don't think he's coming back," he says. "Not anytime soon."

Jill appears beside him and gasps when she sees the carnage in the bathroom. "Oh jeez, Pete," she says. "I hope he's okay."

Pete glares at her. "He *did* hit me with the TV," he says.

"So?" Jill says. "*You're* fine, *he* might not be." Then she shakes her head and sighs. "You guys probably aren't getting your security deposit back."

She looks sidelong at Pete for a moment, then smiles and playfully shoves him.

"Laugh it up, fuzzball," Pete says. "Losing that deposit is the *real* tragedy here." He ruffles her hair and walks into his bedroom, pulls a suitcase out from beneath the bed and starts filling it with clothes. Jill enters Auger's room with her hands in her pockets, looking over the spilled box of jewelry, the operating table, the stacks of notebooks piled on the plastic covered floor.

"*The batcave*," she says to herself. She bends over to pick up a composition book labeled *Maps*, the one containing Auger's plotted routes. She starts thumbing through it, chewing her lip again as she turns the pages. Pete comes in from the hall, suitcase in hand, and peers over her shoulder.

"Auger's treasure maps?" he asks.

"Yep," she says, then tucks the book underneath her arm and turns towards him. "So, are you ready to go?"

Pete blinks. "Go where?"

Jill rolls her eyes. "Well, we have to leave soon to catch the *bus*, and we can't let Mr. Body Bags sit in your trunk for too much longer before someone notices. There was a house in the neighborhood that I used to live in where this guy killed his wife and rolled her up in a rug in the closet and just let it sit there for *days*. He got busted when people called the cops about the smell."

"Huh," Pete says, momentarily bewildered.

"Yep," Jill continues, "and when they arrested him, he was out front cutting the grass. He didn't want it to seem like anything was out of the ordinary."

"So we should cut the grass? I'm confused."

"No, retard, we have to *move* the body," Jill groans. "As in *get rid of it*. Auger's already done all the work for us." She pats the notebook, nestled safely in the crook of her right arm. "We just have to follow whatever route he was planning on using next and we'll be fine."

"Are you serious?" Pete says incredulously. "No, we're not doing that. I don't mind letting Auger get caught on his own, but we're not going to dump a *dead body* for him, that's crazy."

Jill shrugs. "Fine, leave it in your car then. Or you can call the police. Either way we'd both go to jail."

"*Why* would we both go to jail?" Pete asks, then stops, uncertain. "Would we?"

Jill nods authoritatively, despite not actually knowing the answer herself. "Yep," she says. "As accomplices."

"*Shit*," Pete says. "Why couldn't Auger have bought his *own* car? He spent enough money to have *M.A.S.H.* in his bedroom, you'd think a *car* might've been on his shopping list somewhere."

Jill sniffs and raises her eyebrows expectantly.

"Fine," Pete relents. "I suppose we're going to jail no matter what we do, so let's go catch the bus."

"Good idea!" Jill says with an animated nod. "Let's go!" She reaches out and zips Pete's jacket back up, then kisses him lightly on the cheek. "Don't forget

98

your deodorant," she says. "I'm tired of finding hairs in mine."

Afternoon

Pete sits on the couch in Jill's house while she stands in the kitchen assembling peanut butter sandwiches. She is leaving out the jelly for now because its resemblance to the entrails strewn about the inside of Auger's chest freezer is still fresh in her mind.

"Do you like apples?" she asks Pete, tentatively reaching for the fruit in question stored in a bowl on the kitchen counter. "I was going to cut some up."

Pete barely looks up. He has been fanatically checking the clock over the VCR ever since they got back to Jill's house. "Yea, sure, apples are fine," he says. "When do you want to leave?"

Jill sighs, because he has asked some form of this question no less than fifteen times this afternoon. "As soon as it's dark, Pete," she replies, snatching an apple from the bowl and cutting it into sections to slip into a Ziploc bag. "Maybe around six?"

Pete nods to himself. "Do you think we should cover up my license plates with some trash bags or something?" he asks. "Or maybe take them off and put fake ones on? That might be a good idea."

Jill takes some plastic bags out of a counter drawer and slides it shut. "I don't know," she says, "a car with no tags might be *more* suspicious, don't you think? Just, you know, obey the speed limit and everything. We'll be okay."

Pete makes an exasperated groan. "It's not like we're driving around with overdue videotapes, Jillybean," he says. "I'm just nervous, I'm sorry."

Jill wraps the sandwiches in plastic and puts them and the apple slices into a grocery bag. She quickly washes her hands in the kitchen sink and then walks over to the couch where Pete is sitting, wiping her palms on the front of her pants. She flops down next to him, folding her legs underneath herself.

"Look," she says, "it's totally understandable to be nervous, but try to calm down a *little*. We just follow the maps and drop Mr. Man off bit by bit like the airport shuttle bus. Don't speed or swerve and we'll be fine, nothing to worry about." She pats him on the arm excitedly. "Plus, I made *sandwiches!*"

Pete raises an eyebrow at her. "You are *way* too excited about this," he says.

"Yea, well, I can either frown all day or be excited about going on an adventure with my..." Jill stops, suddenly cautious. "You know, with my *friend*," she continues hesitantly.

Pete laughs. "You're afraid to say *boyfriend*, aren't you?" he says. "You're worried about *that*, but not about driving all over the county with pieces of a dead guy in our trunk. You make no sense, madam."

"Shut up!" Jill says. "What *should* I call you? 'Boy who won't leave my house'?"

Pete smiles despite his nerves. "I think 'boyfriend' works," he says. "Unless you wanted to call me 'Batman'."

"Wow, forget I even said anything," Jill says. "You don't get a sandwich now. You can sit in the backseat by yourself."

"It's my car!" Pete protests. "And I don't think either of us is going to feel like eating anyway. I doubt the smell has gotten *better* since this morning."

Jill looks over her shoulder into the kitchen, at the cabinet beneath the sink. "I think we have some air freshener we could bring," she says. "Unless my *boyfriend* thinks we should just drive with all the windows down."

"Your boyfriend thinks we should do both," Pete says, pulling her forward into his lap. "It's supposed to be retarded cold tonight, so we should bring a couple of extra jackets or blankets or something. I'll still run the heater, but it's probably going to smell pretty ripe, like a fart in a jar on a hot day."

Jill laughs and settles into Pete's embrace, clasping her hands over top of his as they rest on her chest. "You are a special guy," she says.

"Thanks," Pete says. "Now since I'm going to be driving, that leaves you on spray detail."

She cranes her neck back to look up at him. "Spray detail?" she asks with a smile.

"Yea, you know, Glade or Febreze or whatever," Pete says. "Anything you have around the house, even a scented *candle* if you promise not to set my front seat on fire."

Jill's eyes widen. "Ooh, maybe we should just *burn* your car. Or push it into a trash compactor like in *Goldfinger*."

Pete blinks. "Let's not deviate from Auger's crazy play book," he says. "We're both smart people, but we're not exactly old hands at corpse-tossing. I'm already pretty sure you and I are going to jail, but if we try to come up with our own plan I am confident we will go to jail *faster*."

Jill sighs and motions for Pete to lean down, then kisses him for a long time. "Do you really think we're going to get arrested?" she asks.

Pete nods, their faces almost touching.

"You seem pretty calm about it," Jill continues. "Much more than you were back at the apartment, anyway."

"Well," Pete says. "I've been experiencing a lot of clarity as of late. The very real prospect of serious jail time is just adding to it, in a way."

Jill chews her lip. "I don't think I understand," she admits.

"Sort of like a near death experience," he says.

"Hey, I've had one of *those*," Jill says, "but I still don't get what you mean."

Pete shrugs. "Well, being faced with your own mortality and finally having to recognize that everything about you is finite. It's a pretty surreal feeling, I'm not doing a very good job of explaining myself."

Jill shakes her head slightly, their noses brushing. "No, I think I've got it," she says. "'Get busy living or get busy dying'."

Pete thinks about this for a moment. "Yea, basically," he says. "Like you said earlier, I can frown about it all day long or I can accept it. I might as well start trying to accept it."

Jill smiles. "There you go," she says. "And plus, you've got *me* to kick around."

"Yea," Pete smiles back. "Prison will give our relationship an interesting opportunity to mature in ways we never would have expected. For example, I can make you a license plate for Valentine's Day."

Jill laughs and playfully bites the tip of Pete's nose. "Maybe we can correspond about our book," she says. "Like, I write a chapter and send it to you, and then you write a chapter and send it back. We can be pen pals."

"That could work," Pete says. "It doesn't really matter what we write about, our situation alone would make us *irresistible* to publishers."

"I know, right?" Jill says. "I never would've thought that jail could be so lucrative. I kind of *want* to go, now."

"I'd still rather avoid it. It doesn't look so great on most *other* job applications. And you know how I've been holding out for a management position at The Loaf."

Jill nods quietly, lost in thought for several moments and looking around at spots on the ceiling above her. "I have a proposition for you," she says at last.

"Okay," Pete says with a trace of uncertainty. "What is it?"

"If we don't go to jail, we both quit The Loaf."

"And do what?" he asks, a quizzical look on his face. "I mean, I know we both hate it, but what would we do for money?"

"Find other jobs," she says. "We get the hell out of here and do something else. We can find an apartment somewhere and split the rent, it wouldn't be that bad. We just try something *new* for a change. If you really want to get busy living, you can't stay for another year at a job you hate taking classes you don't go to for a degree you can't decide on. And honestly, I think cutting and running is *way* less scary than *jail*, so if you can get through this I think you owe it to yourself to change your life. I do."

Pete is silent for a minute. "Wow," he says. "You've really thought about this, haven't you?"

Jill nods. "Yea, I have. And I'm not just trying to project what *I* want onto you, I swear I'm not. I honestly feel like we both need the same things." She sighs and squeezes his hands gently. "And I think we need each other's help. I mean, I *know* I need your help, I think I've known it for a little while now. I thought…" Jill stops, giving a small nervous laugh. "I thought you might need *my* help, too," she says.

Neither person speaks for some time, both of them skillfully avoiding eye contact with each other. Pete focuses back on the VCR clock, the little green dots blinking dutifully in between the hours and minutes, keeping pace with his heart like a metronome. He can feel Jill's hands start to tremble slightly, still wrapped beneath his own on her chest. Pete looks down at her, her face turned away from him and faint tears beginning to form in her eyes.

"I'm sorry," Jill says, still looking away. "That was *way* too much, I'm really sorry."

Pete kisses her on the cheek. "No it wasn't," he says.

Jill turns her head back to face him, her hands tightening almost imperceptibly in his grasp.

"I don't disagree with anything you said," Pete continues. "I think you're right. I think we *do* need the same things. And I think I need you, too."

Jill smiles, her eyes still somewhat red. "Awesome," she says.

Pete looks back at the clock and then out the window at the evening sky. "We have about an hour until it gets dark, I think. Is there anything you'd like to do before we probably go to jail?"

Jill shakes her head. "I can't think of a thing."

"Okay," Pete says. "We'll just stay here then."

They sit entwined on the couch as the light fades slowly through the room with the setting sun.

Pete

One

It was actually about two more hours before it got completely dark outside, but Jill and I barely moved from our positions on the couch. I don't think either one of us really believed it would be the last quiet afternoon we'd get to spend together, but we didn't say another word about it. It's funny, even though I spent all that time talking about realizing the finite nature of life, it still didn't keep me from wishing we never had to get up from that couch.

We went through the house, starting with the cleaning supplies underneath the sink in the kitchen, and tried to assemble everything we thought might be useful. I found coats and blankets in a closet on the second floor, and Jill managed to locate one and a half spray bottles of Febreze after scouring the kitchen, the laundry room and all the bathrooms. We put vinegar and bleach into a box, along with several bottles of water, a flashlight and some liquid detergent. I'm not sure how useful any of it will be, but I've never made a utilitarian list of body-disposal materials before so I just went with what seemed to make sense. This is in addition to the food that Jill packed, along with some separate water bottles specifically for us to drink. She really wanted to make a mix CD for the occasion, and even though I agreed it would be morbidly appropriate, I made her relent to just bringing along whatever music she could decide on quickly since we didn't have the time for her to properly construct a good compilation.

The first stop on Auger's route was about forty minutes away, and there were three more stops afterwards, each in separate cities almost 60 miles apart. This would unquestionably take all night, so we had to stop to get gas before hitting the interstate. Unfortunately, as I had predicted, the smell in the car was now so bad that we had to sit with the doors open to let it air out for several minutes while Jill and I bombed the interior with Febreze. I really can forget about ever trying to resell it. Not even the Kidney Foundation would accept this thing, every inch of it smells like a graveyard by now. Maybe we *should* burn it after we're finished. I wouldn't even try to collect whatever meager insurance settlement I might get. But then I'd have to start taking the bus to work, and that's just not happening.

Two

I'm standing by my car at the gas pump, holding the nozzle in place because the locks that are supposed to keep the handle depressed never seem to be working when I'm in a hurry. And I'm not trying to catch the 8 o'clock showing of *The Truman Show*, I'm trying to catch the 11 o'clock showing of *Pete Doesn't Go to Jail*. So understandably, I'm a little anxious about wasting time.

Jill is pacing around the car with her hands in her jacket pockets. She didn't want to stay inside the car because after we let loose with all that Febreze, it kind of smells like a big sock. We can't decide whether or not that's worse than smelling like a dead person, but neither scent is particularly relaxing. She walks up beside me and stops, watching the numbered display on the pump tick off the current amount of gallons dispensed.

"Well," she says. "No one seems to notice. So far we're doing pretty well."

"Yea," I say. "We've been on the road for about three minutes. As long as we can keep that record for eight more hours, we'll be free to quit our jobs."

"Small victories, Pete," she says. "I was sort of expecting to see blue and red lights as soon as we walked out the door."

I consider this, because I felt exactly the same way when we left Jill's house. "Yea, I suppose we *have* been pretty lucky so far," I concede. "I mean, all it would've taken would've been for someone to have walked by while we were standing there with the trunk open and you and I would be sharing a toilet with no lid right now."

Jill gently bounces her head off my shoulder in agreement, keeping her hands firmly in her pockets against the cold weather. "See?" she says. "We're doing *great*!"

The pump clicks off as my gas tank finally fills. I top it off with a few more squeezes and then replace the nozzle. "So," I say with a sigh, turning to face Jill. "Are you ready to go?"

"Um, *yes*," she says with a shiver. "It's cold as *balls* out here. Let's get back in your car where there are blankets and a heater."

"Okeydoke," I say, and I open the passenger door for her to get back inside. She hops in and immediately wraps a blanket around herself. I cross around to the driver's side and climb in, turn the key in the ignition and pull away from the gas station.

"You know, decomposing bodies generate heat," Jill says as we get on the road heading towards the interstate. "Maybe we should move a leg up here or something."

"I think maybe you should just wait for the car to warm up," I say, wind roaring through the open windows as we pick up speed.

"Maybe we can roll the windows up?" she offers. "It doesn't smell *that* bad in here anymore."

"I have a feeling that won't last, but we can try it," I say. "At least leave them cracked."

She nods and puts the windows back up, leaving about an inch of an opening in each one. We both sit silently for a few moments, tentatively smelling the air as the heater kicks in and we make it to the interstate.

"It's not *too* bad," Jill says. "It kind of smells like you left a smoothie in here for a few days, but it isn't unbearable."

She's right; the air *does* carry the faintest hint of rotten fruit. "Okay," I say, "but you're still on spray detail. If the stink gets to be too much, you have to hose us down again."

Jill nods. "Aye, cap'n," she says, then reaches under her seat for a CD.

"What do you have?" I ask as she slides the disc into the player.

"The Birthday Massacre," she says. "I figure it's moody enough. I brought more CDs if you want something different."

"No, that's fine," I tell her. This is an album I know pretty well so I think it'll help relax me. The familiar opening track begins as we travel onward into the night.

Three

"Okay, we turn right up here," Jill says, her focus alternating between the narrow country road spread out before us and the notebook lying open in her lap. We're been driving for about an hour but it's still pretty early in the night, not quite 9 o' clock. Jill had to do a small amount of spraying after a while because the fruit odor, while not necessarily getting worse, was starting to give me a headache. She's been following the routes planned out in Auger's notes, reading beneath the flashlight because we both figured that would attract less attention than if we were riding around with the interior lights on.

I nod and take the next right hand turn we come across, pointing the car down another stretch of unlit back road. I wonder how Auger even *found* any of the places he put in his book. I imagine him driving around, *in my car* no less, aimlessly looking for good spots to toss a body part or two. Did he look at maps beforehand and try to narrow down remote locations? Did he monitor the news for weeks afterward, checking to see if any of his deposits had been stumbled upon? I feel like Jill and I are anthropologists, trying to reconstruct Auger's behavior based on things he left behind in his room hundreds of years ago. So much of this is a shot in the dark, pun intended because the fact that it's nighttime seems to make it even more of a mystery.

We finally reach the next mile post and I pull the car over, careful not to drive into a ditch running alongside the road. I turn to Jill and ask, "Now what?"

She peers at the notebook, flashlight in hand. "Uh, he doesn't say," Jill answers. "I guess he figured it was dumb to leave instructions for himself."

I frown. This is probably something we should've thought about before we drove all the way out to our first stop. Jill and I are both pretty sharp, but it would seem that when it comes to criminality, we are a pair of *clownshoes*.

"So…" Jill says, turning in her seat and clicking the flashlight off. "What do we do? Just unload a couple of arms or something?"

"Uh, I don't know," I say, struggling to think of a good idea. "Maybe bury them?"

"We don't have a shovel," Jill groans. "*Dammit*, that's such an *obvious* thing to bring, too! Are there wolves or something out here we can feed arms to?"

I look around outside the car, but the blackness seems to stretch on forever. This is some kind of farmland, but I can't see a barn or a tree line anywhere. No visible signs of life. "I don't see anything," I say.

"*Shit*," Jill breathes. She tucks the flashlight under her arm and unbuckles her seatbelt. "Well, pop the trunk I guess," she tells me.

"What? Why? Do you have an idea?"

She shrugs. "I say we each just grab a bag and start walking. Maybe we'll find a pipe or a creek or something."

"Or Jason Vorhees," I say. "We have no idea where we are."

"Look, Pete, *we're* the scary murderers out here tonight," Jill says. "*We* are the ones carrying a chopped-up dead man in plastic bags. If there's anyone out there, they should be afraid of running into *us*."

She's right. It's not like I have a better suggestion. "Okay," I say, pressing the button on my console to unlock the trunk. "Arms it is."

Four

Night outdoors is *dark*. You forget it when you spend your whole life in the city, but go on a camping trip or drive out to the country where there aren't any lights for miles and you will get a stern reminder that after sunset, *you can't see anything*. I've almost tripped five times and we've barely been walking for as many minutes. I'm carrying two plastic-wrapped arms, which are amazingly heavy and painfully odorous, while Jill trudges ahead of me with the flashlight. She really wanted to help me with the carrying, but you would be surprised how much dead weight truly weighs. Besides, there's something chivalrous about insisting upon carrying *both* decomposing limbs. I feel like part of King Arthur's court right now.

So far we have spotted nothing that looks promising, just an endless flat field whereupon the owners seem to be farming dirt and sticks and the occasional beer can. Jill is trying to use the flashlight as sparingly as possible, which I completely agree with. A disembodied beam of light floating across an empty field is excruciatingly suspicious.

Suddenly, Jill stops. "Wait," she says, sniffing the air. "Do you smell that?"

Luckily she cannot see my expression in the dark. "Um, *yes*," I say. "I smell it."

She shakes her head vigorously. "No, not the *arms*," she says. "I smell *animals*. Like farm animals."

I stop and try to get a whiff of what she's talking about, but all I can detect is rancid flesh. "Sorry, I think the scent of death is permanently lodged in my nose."

Jill shushes me. "Listen," she says, and I do as I'm told.

It definitely sounds like animals, a sort of disinterested mass grunting from somewhere ahead of us. Jill starts walking carefully towards the noises, and I do my best to follow without falling and breaking my ankle.

A farm, like Jill thought. Spread out in front of us are a barn, a house, a few other low-lying buildings and several animal enclosures fenced in with big wooden posts. The grunting seems to be coming from the pen closest to us, so we gingerly make our way to the fence and Jill peeks inside.

"Oh yes," she whispers. "*Pigs*."

She turns to me and I can tell despite the darkness that she is grinning like an idiot.

Five

We've gone back to the car to retrieve the legs and I'm currently carrying them back to the farm, following Jill's lead as she almost skips along the field.

"Why wouldn't he just dump the *whole body* here?" she is saying, almost giddy with the relief that our ordeal may be over as soon as it began. "Did you see how fast they ate those arms? They're like *piranhas.*"

It had been quite a sight to see. These are pretty sizeable pigs, about seven in all and each around two or three feet at the shoulder. After only a few minutes they had consumed both plastic packages, bones and all. To be honest, I'd been asking myself the same question as Jill. The pigs seemed too good to be true.

"I almost want to leave the farmer a note," Jill says. "Or a pie or something. Don't farmers like pies?"

"I think so, as long as they're left on a windowsill to cool," I say, shifting the weight of the legs further up my shoulder. I'm really starting to ache from the effort, but admittedly I feel Jill's enthusiasm. I can see the farm ahead of her, and more importantly the pigs' enclosure to her right. The muscles in my arms are burning, crying out like they can see the pigs themselves and know that I'm about to drop this heavy thing I've been carrying. Don't get your hopes up, boys, we've still got another trip after this one.

We get to the fence and Jill helps me heave the legs inside, one after another. The pigs are hesitant this time though, nosing lazily at the lumps we've just tossed down to them.

"Come on, pig," Jill says. "*Eat!*"

The pigs do not obey. In fact, they give no indication they're even paying Jill any attention.

"Maybe they don't like it," I say. "Maybe attempted rapists taste bad."

Jill groans quietly. "How come we find the *finicky* pigs?" she asks.

"Do pigs normally eat dead things?" I honestly don't know the answer, but I seem to remember that there *are* certain types of animals that won't eat something if it's already dead.

"They ate the *arms*," Jill points out. "They eat *tomato cans*, don't they?"

"I think that's goats," I say.

"Well, are there any *goats* here?" Jill asks, looking around the farm.

"*Shit.*"

"Do you see a harvester or a wood chipper anywhere?" I offer, immediately regretting how stupid I just made myself sound. I might as well have asked if she'd spotted a fucking *beaver*.

"That's a *terrible* idea, Pete," Jill says, "there would be dead guy all over the place like rice at a wedding."

"I agree, I just wasted seconds of my life saying that aloud," I say. "I'm sorry."

"Don't apologize, just help me *think*," Jill says, chewing her lip like she always does when she's trying to focus. The pigs are starting to make quite a bit of noise. I'm hoping the commotion doesn't bring anyone outside.

"I think we need to open the bags," I say, staring through the fence at the two black shapes on the ground. "When we put the arms in, the bags were open a little. Maybe they can't tell that there's food inside."

Jill looks back at me in the dark. "Okay, let me see if I can reach them," she says, and lies down on her stomach in front of the enclosure. "I think I can get my arm through the bottom far enough to open them."

There's an alarm ringing in my head right now, pounding my brain against the side of my skull. Without really thinking, I snatch Jill by the back of her jacket and yank her away from the fence, losing my balance and falling on my butt next to her in the process.

"*What're you doing?*" she hisses.

"Think about what we're up to out here," I snap. "I really don't feel like feeding *two* people to pigs, okay?"

Jill stops, having not considered this.

"Look," I continue, standing up and helping her back to her feet, "let's just be a little more cautious. Maybe we can find a piece of wood, a branch or something, and cut the bags open with *that*."

Jill sighs. "Well the *farmer* must go in there from time to time," she says.

"I really don't think the pigs ate *him*."

"Fair enough, but I don't trust them to make that distinction right now," I say.

"Pete, we don't have time to go hunting for sticks in the dark," Jill says. "We have half of a body still sitting in your car, and your car is still sitting by the side of the road waiting for a state trooper or something to drive by and start poking around." She hands me the flashlight this time and gets back down on her stomach, pushing herself forward towards the pigs.

"Watch them," she says. "I'll do it real quick, okay? I promise I won't let them eat my hand."

Jill stretches her arm out beneath the bottom rung of the fence, reaching for the closest mound of black plastic. Holding my breath, I switch the light on and stare nervously down at her grasping fingers.

Six

"There's a time written next to this one," Jill says, pointing at another route copied down in Auger's notebook. We're back in my car and racing away from the farm as fast as a 1997 Mercury Sable will carry us. She shows me the page, holding the flashlight steady as I try to read it and watch the road at the same time.

Each route in the book is traced on graph paper that Auger affixed to the pages with glue, scribbling in notes along the margins. This particular one is directing us to a spot in a neighboring county a little over an hour away, and scrawled next to the map in Auger's unmistakable hand is the time *11:48 PM*. As before, he offers no further explanation, presumably because he didn't expect anyone else to be reading.

"Well, it's currently 10:15," I say, "so we're going to have to beat feet a little if we want to make it."

"There's no date or anything," Jill points out, "not even a day of the week."

I shrug. "I don't know, maybe it isn't a schedule. He didn't say anything about the pigs, either."

God bless those pigs, but things had almost ended terribly for us earlier. They were more or less indifferent to Jill at first while she clawed her way towards the two gift-wrapped limbs, but the moment she tore one of the bags open the pigs went *ballistic*. I shot my foot through the fence and kicked one in the snout as it was going for Jill's bandaged wrist, probably smelling the blood. We switched places for the second leg, and to be honest I think I peed my pants a bit reaching for that damn thing in the middle of a feeding frenzy. I could hear Jill start to hyperventilate behind me, the flashlight beam wagging with each rapid breath she sucked in. I finally reached the leg and pulled the plastic open, retracting my hand just in time to avoid a brace of snapping pig jaws. I felt Jill dragging me out even as I frantically tried to push myself away, and a moment later I was on my feet and kissing her as hard as I could.

"Are you okay?" I asked, squeezing her as tight as my arms would allow. I'd seen enough of her blood lately, and the prospect of seeing any more set my heart racing so fast I could barely breathe.

"Yea, yes, are *you* okay?" she said. "Did they get you?"

I hadn't *felt* a pig bite, but I checked to be sure. "No," I told her. "No, they didn't get me, I'm good."

The pigs were making a pretty intense racket at this point, and in response the light in the nearby farmhouse suddenly switched on, glowing like a guard tower in the night.

"*Shit*," Jill said, then bolted away from the fence, tugging me along with her. "Come on, Pete!"

And we ran back to the car, which brings us up to speed, I think.

Auger

One

I take one last look around the apartment to make sure I haven't left anything behind. I've cleaned up all the glass from the television and the shower door and carried all the pieces down to the dumpster, along with the television itself and the emptied chest freezer which I didn't spend much time cleaning after draining the ice. Garbage collectors aren't likely to think the smell it projects or the bits specked inside to be indicative of anything other than grocery meat left untended for too long. My notes are coming with me, as are my operating table and my cot.

I notice that one of my books is missing, specifically the one containing my plotted routes. I assume that Jill and Pete must be using it to try and dispose of the body I left in Pete's trunk. I consider this as I turn off the lights and close the door behind me, absently touching the flawless new surgical saw nestled in the leather wrap beneath my coat.

Jill

One

Okay, so I now officially hate pigs. I'm never watching *Babe* again unless I'm eating like a whole plate of bacon at the same time and hoping the little bastard can see the irony. The smell in Pete's car is still pretty bad, but I just did spray duty again to sort of reset everything so he can drive. Honestly, we need to get this night over with if for no other reason than we're running out of Febreze.

Our next stop has a very cryptic time associated with it, *11:48 PM*, but of course Auger didn't write *anything* to explain what the hell he's talking about. His mind is like a Chinese puzzle box, I swear to God.

We've been chugging along for a while now since we left the farm behind, listening to a CD by Saves the Day (Pete's choice, it was his turn) and discussing the finer points of *Judge Dredd*, which we saw the end of on TV at my house last night. *I* think it's a retarded movie, but he thinks it should be *celebrated* for how stupid it is.

"Look," Pete is saying, "all I need to say is this: Max Von Sydow gets shot by mutants, and Jurgen Prochnow gets his arms ripped off by Armand Assante's robot. Write that sentence down, keep it in your pocket for a few days and then go back and read it again. It will *change your life.*"

"I don't know who either of those people are," I say. "So unless they were both *president* or something, don't count on it."

"Max Von Sydow is the father from *The Virgin Spring*," Pete offers, which actually helps because I *have* seen that movie before. It's this really old black and white movie about a man whose daughter gets raped and murdered by three transients in the woods, and then the three guys unwittingly come to his house and ask to stay the night and he kills all of them. It's pretty gnarly.

"Oh," I say. "You said someone gets his arms ripped off? Do they show it?" We had evidently already missed this part when we tuned in yesterday.

"No, not really," Pete says. "You see some really watery-looking blood hit the floor, but that's all."

"That's dumb. If you're going to have a robot pull someone's arms out in your movie, you should at least let us *see* it."

"Really, if you ever watch it you'll be laughing too hard to complain," he says. "It's *that* amazing."

We're nearing a pretty nondescript exit on the interstate that Auger's notebook is instructing us to take. "Get off here," I tell Pete, pointing to the green sign reflecting in his headlights before us. He flicks the turn signal and steers the car into the off ramp, and once again we find ourselves piloting down some back roads in undiscovered country. Seriously, how the hell did Auger figure all this out? He's like Magellan.

"Does he say what I'm looking for?" Pete asks, turning his high beams on. "Another mile post?"

"A bridge," I read from the notebook. "He says to stop at a bridge.

Evidently it's the only one on this road, it intersects after about 20 miles."

Pete nods. "We still have a little bit of time," he says. I look at the clock on his radio and it's reading *11:02*, so we have like forty five minutes to make it to see whatever Auger was talking about. After the pigs, I really can't say what I'm expecting. Maybe there's a troll underneath this bridge that's going to eat the rest of the dead body parts we've got, I don't know.

We drive on for a while pretty much silent, listening to Pete's Saves the Day album. It's been an interesting night, to say the very least. But at the same time, I feel like I'm really *enjoying* myself, you know? Not in a weird I-like-dead-people sort of way, but like in a Bonnie and Clyde way. Pete and I are kind of like them, I think, or like that Steve Miller song about Billy Joe and Bobby Sue. The romanticized bandits, risking everything just to be together. It's *exciting*, to be perfectly honest. I don't recommend ever trying something like it if you absolutely don't *have* to, but I feel like the experience is going to do wonders for our relationship, at least as far as establishing a good foundation. I mean, we can't *help* but completely trust each other after something like this, and they say the first few months are the most important for laying the groundwork of a long-term commitment. At least, that's what I've *heard*.

Ugh, spray duty again. It smells like Charles Barkley's foot locker in here. I empty the last of the Febreze, then lean over and kiss Pete for a minute. He loses an eyelash in the exchange, which I wipe up on my index finger and blow into the air, privately wishing that we don't end up in jail over this. Eyelash wishes are serious business, so I hope someone was paying attention.

Two

"I think that might be it," Pete says, pointing ahead through the windshield down the road in front of us. I look and see the cris-crossing patterns of a railway bridge emerging through the dark, raised a good twenty-five feet above us on strong steel legs to carry passing trains safely overhead. He pulls the car over into a patch of grass, and yet again I'd like to point out that there are no *streetlights* anywhere. But that's probably why Auger picked these spots, so I can't really complain about it.

Pete flicks on his emergency blinker just in case some drunk should come swerving his pickup down the dusty road behind us, and we sit in silence for a few seconds listening to the lights tick over and over. I'm having one of those moments where you think about every memory you have, from growing up to earlier in the week, and then you realize that each one of those memories has brought you to exactly where you are right now. Each one was a stepping stone, a catalyst, pushing you forward towards this *now* that you're currently experiencing. Every birthday, every kiss, every time I stubbed my toe has been carrying me inexorably towards sitting in this car with Pete in front of a bridge with half of a dead rapist in the trunk, listening to the clicking of the hazard lights as they blink on and off. This is my life, how do you do?

"I think we'll probably see a train go by at 11:48," Pete says.

I'm sure that he's right.

Three

We're carrying a bagged torso up a steep embankment towards the bridge. I think I've got the lower end, but honestly, with so many stumps it's hard to tell just by touch. And it is *heavy*. I had no idea how heavy dead stuff could be. I have so much more respect for those guys that put bodies into body bags and then stick them into ambulances. That must be a *killer* workout.

I should point out that Pete and I haven't really decided what we're going to do when the train shows up. I think Auger would toss the remains into an open car as it passes by, but Pete is pretty gung-ho about leaving it on the tracks to get pulverized beneath the wheels. Honestly, we're probably going to do Pete's idea, because I'm not sure I can swing this thing into a moving train. Like I said, I'm built like a pixie stick, so I just don't think I have it in me. How Auger managed to do all of this by himself is something I'll never understand. He must eat a can of spinach before each stop.

I slip on some gravel near the top of the embankment and my end of the body goes sliding down, taking Pete off balance. He almost falls along with it, but he digs his heels into the ground and holds tight. I curse and stoop down to pick my end up, trying to avoid Pete's eyes because I can feel that he's glaring at me a little and I'm genuinely somewhat ashamed. Bonnie and Clyde *never* had this problem, I guarantee.

"I'm a *girl*," I say, snatching up the end of the package that I'd dropped. "I'm sorry I'm not built like a *fireman*, excuse me."

Pete sighs. "I didn't say anything," he says. "Just be careful, I don't want either of us tripping down this hill and breaking a leg. The drive home is going to be hilarious enough."

"Yea, I know, I brought a Louis C.K. CD," I say, smiling sidelong at him until he notices and laughs too. The stupid jokes are the most fun, in my book. After some shuffling, grunting and groaning, we get the son of a bitch back into the air again and lay it across the train tracks at the top. I look down through the slats and see a quarry below, running beneath the roadway Pete stopped his car along. I bet people sleep down there sometimes, waiting for a train to come by and take them to the next state or something. I have a very *Grapes of Wrath* image in my mind right now, which I'm sure is nothing close to accurate but I hang on to it anyway, picturing a man with a broken stove-pipe hat feeding a three-legged dog from a tin can of baked beans, nestled around a fire underneath the bridge.

"So we just leave it here?" I ask, still staring between the slats, my palms wrapped around two lengths of splintered wood as my eyes peek through like Anne Frank watching from her secret attic. "Do we have to angle it a certain way or something?"

"I'm not sure," Pete says, circling the package and nudging it into different positions with his foot. "I suppose horizontal to the tracks? That would pretty much crush the whole torso. Anything that doesn't get totally destroyed will be flung down under the bridge and eaten by animals, I think."

I nod, still focused at the imaginary world I've created in the quarry below. "How much time do we have?" I ask him.

Pete stops, and I realize that I don't have a watch or a cell phone either. "Ah, I don't know," he says, and almost in response we feel the bridge begin to shake like an afternoon in California as a train whistle sounds close by. I spring to my feet and see that Pete is already running towards me, reaching out his hand to grab mine. I jump and he snatches me to him and we both go flying down the embankment, scraping ourselves up on gravel and God knows what else while the train goes thundering across the bridge above us, it's so *loud* I can't believe it, it sounds like a tornado is rushing by and when we hit the road we just lay there, Pete with his arms wrapped around me like he's afraid something is going to come and take me away from him forever. Finally the train passes by and the noise dies down until we're both just lying alone on a dark country mile.

"Jill," Pete says, breathing heavily into my neck as he clings to me like a Koala bear.

"Yes?" I say.

"Let's get the hell out of here."

"Okay," I say, and he pulls me to my feet. I stand staring at the bridge for another couple of seconds, thinking about the hobo and his three-legged dog, Anne Frank and all of my birthdays.

"What's up?" Pete asks, taking my hand in his.

"Nothing," I say. "Life is just pretty fucking weird sometimes." I turn to him. "Do you want to stop at a Waffle House? I could kill a man for some breakfast food right now."

Pete laughs. "Sure, okay. I think we might have to burn my car though."

I shrug. "That's fine, Waffle House is open all night. We can torch the fucker after I get my smothered and covered hashbrowns."

Four

So I'm finally getting to meet Pete's friend Nick, and he seems really great. We're standing inside the Blockbuster Video where Nick works, looking out the wide storefront windows as Pete's car smolders down to embers, and Nick doesn't seem to care at all. He's just sipping a bottle of Diet Coke next to us, watching the hunk of junk burn. It's way past closing time so there's no one else around to bother us or freak out or anything.

"You don't mind calling the cops?" Pete asks him.

Nick shakes his head. "No, what do I care? I just tell them you guys came to visit me at closing and then WOOSH! Your car goes up, probably some crackheads or something." He shrugs, taking another swig of soda. He reminds me of what Steve Zahn probably looked like ten years ago. "As long as you help me vacuum, I don't mind."

I give Nick a big goofy hug, because I feel such a thing is totally appropriate for the situation. "*Good to meet you*," I say to him. He gives me kind of a weird look but pats my shoulder to reciprocate.

"Yea, you too," he says. "Pete talks about you all the time."

I flash an *oh really* look at Pete, and he turns about eleven shades of red. "All good things, I hope," I say.

"Oh definitely," Nick says, walking towards the back of the store to start his closing duties. "I'm just glad you guys are finally dating. I thought I was going to have to kidnap him and, like, ask you out *in disguise*."

We showed up here about twenty minutes ago and convinced Nick to let us inside, since he had already locked the doors for the night. Pete gave a real superficial explanation about why we needed to burn the car, something about borrowing against it for his student loans, and then Nick helped us cover it with a can of gasoline he had in his own car and set it on fire. He didn't even bat an eyelash, I don't think. We probably could've asked for his help dumping body parts earlier tonight if he hadn't been at work.

"Is that going to be dangerous at all?" Pete asks, staring at his flaming Sable. "I mean, is it going to explode?"

I shrug. "I wouldn't think so, but if it does there aren't any other cars near it. We can call the police and the fire department in a minute, I guess."

"Yea, we can do that," Nick says from the back, rustling through a closet for cleaning supplies. "I mean, *I* have to park across the street, so that thing can blow up like Nakatomi Plaza for all I care, it won't affect me."

We decide to let it just keep burning, and after helping Nick clean up the video store we walk a few blocks down the road to Waffle House, leaving Pete's flaming car behind for someone else to report. By that time, any incriminating evidence will probably be gone, and we can say we just parked it there to meet Nick before going to Waffle House and that we have no idea what happened. I should write that down in Auger's notebook for him, just in case we ever get the chance to give it back. He'd probably appreciate some new ideas.

Pete

One

I checked in with my landlord yesterday after Jill and I had slept in for ten hours to let her know that I would be moving out at the end of our lease, which expires in another month. But when I did, she told me that Auger had already severed our lease and paid a penalty fee a day before, and she let me into the apartment to clear all my stuff out while simultaneously stressing the fact that I didn't *technically* have to be moved until the end of the month although it would be appreciated. With Jill's help, I packed everything I had left in my room into some cardboard boxes that my landlord had in her office (probably squirreled away for the occasional eviction, but whatever, I'll take what I can get) and took it back to her house. Auger had already removed all of his stuff as well as the things we'd broken during our fight a few nights before. I swear I will never understand the way his mind operates.

Jill's parents come home in a few days. After moving me out of the apartment, the two of us spent about forty five minutes on the phone with them, pleading our case. We really tried to play the angle that Auger had totally ditched me for no reason and I was stuck without a way to pay my rent, an experience they could both relate to having been teenagers in the 70's. Jill's mom said that, by the way. Personally I have no idea why the decade would make a difference, but I'm trying to move into my girlfriend's parents' house, so I just sort of agreed with everything positive that I heard. Eventually they relented and said they'd let me stay, though her father was pretty insistent that I have my own room and that I pay some kind of rent, which I totally agree with. I actually would have insisted on paying rent if they hadn't brought it up themselves. Also, it helped that her parents have met me several times before and already think I'm the cat's pajamas, especially Jill's mom. If the girl's mom likes you, you're in. That's just a fact.

We're riding the bus right now, huddled against each other because it's like John Carpenter's *The Thing* outside. I got some real cursory questions about my car catching fire the other night, but the cops didn't seem terribly concerned about it, particularly after I said I wasn't looking for any insurance since the vehicle was thirteen years old. Nick was a huge help too, perfectly corroborating our story to the police. He made us both promise to invite him out to wherever we end up, which I have no problem with. He's an interesting guy, you could probably write a book about *him* if you really wanted.

The bus is lumbering along, Jill is sitting in my arms, I love her more than anything and for the first time since I can remember I'm truly, solidly happy. Excited about the future. I feel like my life is about to turn a major corner. I guess I just have to wait and see.

Last Day

Jill wraps a bagel for the customer at the bakery register and hands it to him, thanking him for stopping by and wishing him a good day at work. The man smiles and reciprocates the sentiments with a nod, then turns around and walks out of The Loaf. Jill sighs, having no other customers in line, and looks over at Pete on the other side of the restaurant, preparing the deli portion of the store for the impending lunch rush. She smiles at him, then wipes her hands on her apron and goes to refill the bagel trays with fresh product pulled from the ovens in the back, quietly singing a song to herself and imagining what it will be like to live in her parents' house with her boyfriend. Jill brings a tray of bagels to the front to unload them into the bakery display but stops when she notices a customer standing at her register. It is the man that she and Pete have dubbed Foggle, the free-sample thief clutching a canvas bag of his ill-gotten gains from around the neighborhood.

"Good morning, sir," she greets him politely, reciting her daily script. "Can I start you off with a cup of coffee today?"

Foggle nods, reaching into his plastic bag to hand her a 7-11 coffee cup. "In my own cup, if you don't mind," he says. "You never know what goes into those other ones."

Jill accepts the Styrofoam cup without debate, despite the fact that every morning Foggle repeats the same phrase and every morning she thinks to herself *you don't know what's in this cup either, mister*. While filling the cup, she notices a tiny drawing scrawled on the side depicting a toaster with a bandana wielding a sword against an octopus clutching four machine guns and starts laughing uncontrollably.

Jill notices Foggle smiling at her. "You like the picture?" he asks. "I've got a bunch more, someone drew on all my coffee cups. I like it, it's like waking up every morning and reading the comics." He reaches into his bag to pull out a big stack of cups, handing them to Jill tentatively. "You can look at them if you wash your hands, I don't mind."

Jill laughs again. "That's pretty cool," she says. "I don't want to mess your cups up though, it's okay." She hands him his coffee. "Have a good day, sir."

Foggle shrugs and puts the stray cups back into his bag, taking his fresh coffee from Jill with a nod. "James," he says. "My name is James."

Jill doesn't respond for a moment, momentarily dumbstruck by his revelation. "Uh, I'm Jill," she says finally, pointing at her nametag.

Foggle smiles. "I know," he says. "I come in here all the time. Have a nice day, Jill." He turns and walks through the exit, suddenly more grandfatherly than Jill would have ever expected. He holds the door open for someone else, someone that Jill recognizes, but Todd appears behind her and shatters her concentration.

"Pastries need refilling," Todd barks into her ear. "Clean the bread slicer too. This isn't your home, we want people to feel *welcome* here."

"Sure, okay," Jill says, moving away from her register to start restocking the bakery's pastry display. She stacks a row of muffins as high as they can stand without touching the sneeze guard, then grabs a rag from one of the sinks and starts cleaning the bread slicer, all the while thinking about the exchange she just had with Foggle.

"Nice one," she hears Pete say, and turns to see him standing next to her, grinning and holding a massive lump of turkey ready to be portioned. "I guess Foggle liked our drawings."

"Yea, he did!" she says, careful not to cut her finger as she pulls a particularly large chunk of stale bread from the slicer. "And he told me his name was James."

Pete nods. "Huh," he says. "I never would've guessed. I pegged him for a Walt or something. An old man's name."

"Back to the line, Pete," Todd says. "We're an hour from rush and I need you to make it ready. I *don't* need you to stand here and waste time with your girlfriend." Todd shakes his bald, sweaty head. "You're not even supposed to be *dating*."

"The employee handbook says it's fine," Pete says, walking back to the other side of the restaurant. "As a manager, you *should* know that."

Todd points a finger at Pete, trembling slightly. "*You* can come have a talk with me in the back after your shift," he says. "We'll see who knows what."

Pete gives him a little salute in response. Jill turns back to the slicer to try and hide her laughter, dutifully wiping old bread crumbs from between the blades.

"Excuse me," Jill hears a customer say behind her. "Is your name Todd?"

"Yes, I'm Todd, I'm the manager on duty," Todd says, still somewhat flustered over his exchange with Pete. "What can I do for you, sir?"

"Nothing at all." There's a familiar quality to the man's voice, a distant scratchiness that Jill feels she knows. *Like a robot*, she thinks, and turns around to see Auger standing in front of the bakery, his face and hands covered in hundreds of cuts, and she can tell that he's wearing his tools beneath his jacket but the thing about his appearance that concerns her the most is that he is actually *smiling*, his teeth shining white through a pair of shredded lips.

"Auger?" she says, and he looks at her, the smile growing slightly.

"Hi Jill," he says, and suddenly his arms explode forward and grab Todd by the neck. He's holding a big saw, it looks brand new compared to the broken one he wielded in the apartment the other night, and she cries out and stumbles backwards as Auger drags the teeth across the back of Todd's neck with a brutal stroke. She hears a snapping sound like a wet stick as Auger pulls the saw once more, and Todd's body shudders to the floor, a geyser of blood spraying from the stump that is his neck. Auger turns and lobs Todd's severed head into the newspaper rack by the front door, people are beginning to notice what's happening and Jill hears a lady start to scream. Auger looks back at her, the smile is gone but there's something reassuring about the look on his mutilated face, and when she tries to speak to him she finds that she cannot. He moves quickly behind the counter, his jacket and exposed leather tool wrap now covered in blood, and heads towards the deli.

Towards Pete.

Jill calls out, trying to get Pete's attention because he hasn't seen Auger yet, he just came in from the back with that idiot Jake and they're setting up the soup station. Pete looks up with a quizzical expression, but when he sees Auger his face drops and he starts scrambling backwards. Auger reaches them and smashes his elbow into Jake's cheek, then delivers a backhand that sends Jake to the floor. He grabs Pete by the shoulders and slams him against the deli counter, and Pete is still too stunned to react, his hands are raised palm open in the air. Auger snatches a long chef's knife lying nearby and flips it deftly in his hand, pointing the blade at Pete's midsection.

"Stand still," Auger says.

Epilogue

Auger sits across from Jill and Pete, dressed completely in white and staring at them through a thick window made of glass and wire. It was a long drive for them across several states, but neither one of them had seen Auger since the day he went to jail and they decided they wanted to have one last friendly encounter before he disappeared from their lives forever. They waited patiently for five minutes while Auger was brought out of his room, but now with him finally here neither of them can think of anything to say. Pete rubs his scarred stomach absently and gives a nervous laugh.

"So, uh, how are you?" he asks.

Auger shrugs.

Jill looks down at her hands, fidgeting a moment before speaking. "Are… are they nice to you?"

"They try to be, for the most part," Auger says. "Everyone here is afraid of me, though. I have to spend most of my time by myself."

Jill nods, some small tears beginning to form in her eyes.

"Don't cry, Jill," Auger says, "I don't mind. I get to read. I think they may let me have a pen and paper soon."

Jill laughs a little, and Pete shifts in his seat. "Hey," he says, "you really… you took care of everything. The police only talked to me a couple of times. I didn't even have to pretend to be surprised when they told me you confessed to burning my car."

Auger doesn't say anything. His face is still mapped with scars, but most of them seem to be healing.

Pete says, "You still owe me a kidney. What did you do with it, anyway?"

Auger opens his mouth to respond.

"Nevermind," Pete says quickly. "In light of everything else, I guess we can call it even."

"You can have one of mine," Auger says.

Jill snorts, then covers her face with her hands and looks sheepishly at the other two.

Auger leans forward slightly and asks, "Did you get any money from work?"

Pete and Jill share a glance before Pete responds. "Yea, some," he says. "We took it and moved away as soon as the cops said it was alright to leave the state."

"Where did you go?"

Jill starts to speak but Pete shakes his head and stops her. "Up north," he says.

Jill tries to smile but it quickly falters. "You know, we probably can't come see you again," she says.

"I know," Auger says, "but I'm glad you did today."

Pete stands and prompts Jill to do the same. "We have to get going," he says. "We have a pretty long drive. Take care of yourself, okay?"

"I will. Stay out of trouble."

Pete laughs and he and Jill start to walk away. Suddenly Jill stops and rushes quickly back, sliding something to Auger through a narrow slot in the window. Auger looks down to see a tiny red button marked with the words *I Am Loved*.

"Thanks for being my friend," Jill says, her face now streaked with tears. She turns back to Pete and they leave, their footsteps echoing as they depart. Auger discreetly palms the button, not having a pocket to safely store it in as a heavy guard appears next to him and ushers him out of the visiting area into the hallway towards his room. As they walk, Auger squeezes the button tightly in his hand until the metal pin on the back digs into his skin and he smiles.

October 17, 2008 - January 29, 2009

Made in the USA
Lexington, KY
10 March 2014